David M

A MAN of COLOR

DORRANCE
PUBLISHING CO
EST. 1920
PITTSBURGH, PENNSYLVANIA 15238

Dorrance Publishing Co
585 Alpha Drive
Suite 103
Pittsburgh, PA 15238
Visit our website at *www.dorrancebookstore.com*

ISBN: 978-1-6853-7226-2
eISBN: 978-1-6853-7765-6

A
MAN
of
COLOR

To
Dolores & Carl

The sweet tangy aroma of the baked strawberry and rhubarb pies, sitting next to him, on the worn brown leather seat, filled the black man's nostrils, as he drove his '46 GMC pickup along the highway. His employer's wife had baked the pies for him and his family. The writhing scent seduced his senses and caused his mouth to water.

Beneath Zadok's glistening chestnut brown skin, his muscles ached and were taut. But the sensation gratified the man. The sensation reminded him that he had accomplished something, during a hard day's work. He had earned the pay that supported him and his wife and son. And the hard work kept his six foot, four inch frame in good shape. He liked the hard physical labor. About the only thing he liked better was going home, showering, and spending a relaxing evening with his family. And the best thing was crawling into bed, next to his wife, and making love.

A smile spread across Zadok's handsome dark face as he pulled the faded blue pickup onto the dirt road that led to home. In the twilight, the grade gradually steepened then leveled off, just before forking. The man steered the truck to the left. The lane curved and ended in a rough oval, in front of a plain but sturdy house, a refuge from the ordinary mundane concerns of life, a shelter of warmth and contentment. Zadok opened the cab door and stepped out into the dusk. He scooped up the pies in both big hands and, with his boot, shoved the truck door closed. As he strode towards the porch, the man noticed hens roosting on the window sill and the porch swing.

"That boy..." he grumbled.

Before he reached the steps, Zadok noticed the family dog, laid out on his side, at the corner of the porch. His brow furrowed, the man walked over to the still tan hound. The man's stomach fluttered and his face warmed when he noticed that the dog wasn't breathing. Zadok quickly turned, dashed up the steps, hurdling them in one leap, like a panicked jack rabbit, and hit the front door, which was ajar, with his shoulder.

He scanned the dimly lit interior. The coffee table was shoved against the sofa; the lounge chair and the ottoman were overturned near the bookcase. Zadok noticed that the dining table had been pushed against the wall, and a chair was overturned. Flowers, from a fallen vase, were strewn over the hardwood floor. And the throw rug was clumped up in a pile. It was as though a storm had whirled through the house.

The man's heart began thumping. Lunging forward, Zadok tossed the pies at the table, ignoring where or how they landed. He leaped over the ottoman, dashed past the wood stove, and entered the kitchen. The man could hear faint whimpering, like that of a small wounded animal. Halting, Zadok listened for a moment. The sound was coming from the bedroom that he and his wife shared. He felt a cold sweat breaking out on his face and a chill radiated through his body. Zadok dreaded what he suspected.

Approaching the open door, the man could see his wife, kneeling beside the bed, donned only in her camisole and bloomers. He saw his twelve-year-old son lying, supine, on the bed, seemingly in a fitful sleep. The boy's breath was rapid and shallow, his face swollen and bruised. Slowly, Zadok passed through the door and stood over his family. His wife's wavy black hair was mussed about her delicate, sullen face. The man knelt beside her and clasped her golden brown shoulders. She did not respond to his touch.

"Tassy, what happened?" her husband's low voice rasped.

The woman still did not respond. Gently, Zadok squeezed her shoulders and urged her to face him. Tassy vacantly stared at his chest, while her husband peered at the swelling below her right eye and at the dried blood clotted in her split lower lip.

The woman's camisole was torn in the front, revealing her cleavage and her flat stomach. Rage simmered inside of Zadok, like smoldering embers amid ashes. He bared his clenched white teeth.

Gently shaking his wife, the man repeated his question, "Tassy, what happened?

The woman merely responded by raising her somber eyes to her husband's glowering face. Zadok lifted his wife to her feet and urged her to one side. Leaning over the boy, the man scooped up his son into his thick arms. The boy winced with the movement and moaned.

Cradling his son, Zadok summoned his wife. "Tassy."

The woman, lost in her own despair, seemed unaware of his voice.

Her husband barked, "Tassy!"

Startled out of her melancholy, the woman's red eyes darted and focused on Zadok's stern visage.

Her husband ordered her to lead the way to the truck. "We need to get our boy to the doctor!"

For a moment, Tassy was still. But as the demand registered in her clouded mind, she acted. The woman scampered to the gaping front door, down the porch steps and across the yard to the pickup. She climbed into the passenger side of the cab. Zadok was right behind her and lay their son across the seat, the boy's head resting on his mother's lap. The man dashed around the cab and jerked the door open. Lifting his son's feet, Zadok slid into the seat. The engine turned over and growled as the truck eased down the dirt lane. When the pickup bounced or lurched over the rough road, the boy let out gasps and groans.

Zadok hissed a sigh of relief when the truck came to the paved highway. The asphalt seemed to race beneath them. Glancing over to his wife, the man noticed how she silently stared out of the windshield. He turned his eyes back to the highway. Zadok was lost in his own despair and was only subconsciously aware of the countryside they were passing: Tibbideau's sweet potato patch, Black's woods, Pettijohn's corn field, Kendall's pasture land, Anderson's cotton field, Henshaw's peas and green beans, Sample's hog farm, Canby's dairy and Packard's mule farm.

The man was more attentive when they neared town. He slowed down as they passed Darky Town and the nursery on one side of the street, and the lumberyard and the feed store on the other. He exceeded the speed limit on Main Street then braked and took a right on Blue Jay Road, following it to Black Willow Street, where he turned left onto a rough paved lane. Zadok frowned at the large brown house that came into view on his right. He pulled into the gravel driveway and stopped behind the black '50 Chevy Nomad station wagon.

Tassy remained still while her husband leaped from the cab, raced around and flung open the passenger's door. Gently, Zadok gathered up his son and strode to the porch, hopping over the wooden steps. He rapped on the door. While he waited, the man glanced over his shoulder to his wife, who remained rigidly seated in the truck. Zadok rapped again. The door opened, and the visitor faced a lanky, pale, elderly man, equal to his own height, who frowned with uncertainty beneath his thick silver mustache. Donned in a faded maroon house coat, with a frayed black collar, the elder ran his long fingers through his silver hair, then adjusted his wire-rimmed glasses.

His thick knitted brows sprang up with recognition. "Zadok!"

The father pleaded, "Please, doc, my boy is bad hurt!"

The doctor stepped aside, as his visitor rushed through the entry and down the hall.

The physician called out, "The door to your left, Zade!"

The black man entered the examination room and laid his son on the black padded table.

As the doctor entered and stood over the boy, Zadok exclaimed, "I'm going to go get Tassy! She was hurt too!"

He hurried through the hall and out onto the porch, leaping the steps. Upon reaching the truck, Zadok opened the cab door and reached for his wife's hand. She seemed so frail and damaged.

"Tassy," he softly addressed her, "Dr. Orley is going to take a look at you; he's going to help."

With a gentle tug, the man coaxed his wife out of the pickup. He placed an arm around her cringing shoulders and led her up the porch to the door.

In the examining room, they found the doctor gingerly probing along their son's rib cage. The boy let out a weak groan.

Dr. Orley looked up over his glasses and gestured to an adjacent room.

"Take her in there, Zade. I'll tend to her, in a moment."

The physician resumed examining the boy.

Inside the other room, Zadok found a hard-back chair sitting next to another examining table. He urged Tassy to sit in the chair, while the man leaned against the wall, rubbing his fingers across his lower lip and, with anxious concern, gazing on his somber wife. He felt like a kettle sitting motionless on a burner while kernels of corn ricocheted against the interior.

Dr. Orley entered. His narrow shoulders slouched under his robe, and he held up his glasses, wiping the lenses with a handkerchief.

The physician let out a sigh. "Well, Gideon took quite a beating. He has bruises and abrasions over his face, arms, and torso."

Looking over to the withdrawn woman, Dr. Orley moaned.

"Good god, what bastard did this?"

"I don't know," Zadok muttered as he stared at the wall.

Lowering to one knee, the doctor tenderly cradled Tassy's chin between his thin long fingers and gently raised her head, turning it from side to side.

"That's quite a shiner, my girl," Dr. Orley observed. He looked into the woman's lifeless eyes and told her, "Tassy, I'm going to stand you up. I'm going to help you remove your garments. Then I want you to lay on this cot, over here." The physician gave a slight nod towards the padded table. "I want to examine you and figure out the full extent of—well, just get an idea of your condition. Alright?"

She gazed into the doctor's gaunt face, her eyes swollen, red, and distant. Silently, Tassy stood up. And Dr. Orley rose to his feet.

Turning to Zadok, the physician suggested, "Why don't you go look in on your boy? We'll be a few minutes."

For a moment, as he gawked in response, the husband seemed uncertain. But then he gave a nod and stepped out, closing the door behind him. Outside of the room, Zadok stood and thought how fortunate it was, for him and his family, that Dr. Orley had the compassion that a physician should have and was willing to treat colored folks. Black, white, or whatever, people were flesh and bone, feelings and emotions. They were all vulnerable; they all had needs. Beneath the flesh, people all looked the same: red-blooded, white-boned, gray matter, heart, lungs, muscle, and sinew. Any doctor should understand that. Zadok, a black common laborer, did.

Dr. Orley towered over the five foot, four inch frame of his patient. Placing a large slim hand on her back, he directed Tassy to the examining table. As the woman turned and leaned against the foot of the table, the physician gingerly lifted the camisole off of her shoulders and allowed the garment to slide down her shapely arms. Dr. Orley laid the vest over the back of the nearby chair. He waited for his patient to slip out of her bloomers. But she just stood, gazing into space, with her arms folded over her breasts.

Pursing his lips, Dr. Orley delicately gathered the fabric with his fingertips, below her hips, and tugged the underwear down her smooth thighs. Her naked body tensed, as a chill seemed to radiate through her. Releasing the material, the man allowed the bloomers to fall at his patient's feet. Tassy stepped out of the garment.

Softly clasping Tassy's shoulders, Dr. Orley told her, "I need you to hop up, on the cot, and lay down."

With her vacant eyes lowered, the patient complied. Hunched over her, the physician peered into her face. A gentle fingertip traced the bruise under her eye and probed near the cut on her lip. Tender hands slid under her arms and down her sides, gingerly pressing against her ribs. Then, Dr. Orley turned and gathered a pair, of thin rubber gloves, from a box.

As he slipped the gloves over his hands, the man informed the woman, "Tassy, I need you to bend your knees and splay your legs."

Silently and reluctantly, she complied. Tassy felt the hands on her thighs, felt the fingers part her labia. And tears ran down her cheeks and neck. The horrible memory of her attack assailed her mind. The degradation filled her soul, as the physician probed inside of her with a swab.

"I'm so sorry, Tassy," he apologized.

Concluding his examination, the man removed the gloves and, taking his patient's hand, assisted her to sit up and stand. He handed her the garments. After Tassy dressed, the doctor led her to the chair, where she compliantly sat. Dr. Orley knelt before her.

"Tassy, I know you were raped, and I know it was a horrible experience." He rubbed his square chin. "Now I've known you since you were a baby. I've tended to you and your family for years. I know the trauma is painful to deal with. But, Tassy, I need you to tell me just what happened. Who did this to you and to Gideon? What are the details?"

Tassy pulled the plastic curtain aside and stepped out of the shower stall. She began to dry off her wet body. As the woman scrubbed the towel over her damp raven hair, Tassy heard the dog barking outside. Suddenly the sound stopped. Probably just a raccoon or fox, she thought to herself.

Then, beginning to slip into her bloomers, she heard a strange male voice calling. "Yoo-hoo! Anybody home?"

Suddenly, the woman froze in alarm. Was that from inside the house, she feared.

She next heard Gideon's demanding voice. "What do you want?"

"Back off, boy!" a voice grumbled.

Tassy's heart seemed to skip. Was that the same strange voice as the first, or a different one?

"Hey, get out!" her son hollered.

She heard scuffling and banging. There were grunts and yelps.

Quickly, Tassy pulled up her bloomers and pulled on her camisole. Slipping into her light bathrobe, the woman opened the bathroom door to a skirmish; Gideon stood with a chunk of firewood in his hands, and facing three young white men. A tall lanky brunette, in a striped t-shirt and denim trousers, cradled his left arm while grimacing at the threatening boy. Beside the brunette stood a taller, bulkier, tawny-haired man wearing a black and tan jacket. He was chuckling. And, standing apart from the others, was a chestnut-haired boy near a corner, who appeared anxious and reluctant.

The brunette lurched at Gideon. The boy swung his chunk of

wood but missed, as his foe dodged the blow and threw a right hook, bashing Gideon in the cheek. Her son staggered, and his opponent followed with a blow to the boy's ribs.

Tassy cried out as her son dropped to his knees, clutching his side. Her shrill voice drew the intruders' attention. Like hungry wolves, the brunette and the blonde leered at her. And the tall broad young man in the jacket began to approach. The woman was frozen with apprehension. The man gave a lascivious grin. Then, the brunette kicked her son in the stomach. As Gideon gasped and doubled over, the attacker punched his victim twice in the kidney.

His mother shrieked, "Stop!"

She started for her son but was intercepted by the blonde, who grabbed her arm and jerked her back towards him.

He ogled her. "Bernie was right; you ain't bad lookin', for a coon!"

Glaring at the lecherous assailant, Tassy yanked her arm from his grasp. As she scowled, flaring her nostrils, the man slugged her below her eye. A blast of pain shocked her. The woman's face throbbed as her attacker once more grabbed her arm. Tassy struggled. Her abuser back-handed her in the mouth. Then, nearly dragging her, the man strode towards the back of the house and into the bedroom Tassy shared with her husband. The other two intruders followed, the brunette seeming eager and excited, while the other appeared dreadful.

Standing next to the bed, the tawny-haired man ripped open his victim's camisole, tearing the light blue bow and popping the small buttons. He yanked the garment away from her body. The woman's firm golden breasts rose and fell with her rapid breaths, as she concealed them with her folded arms. A crooked smile started on her assailant's lips.

"Looky here, Reg!"

In response, the leering brunette nodded. "Nice tits!"

The big blonde jerked one of her arms away and clutched her breast in his broad hand, kneading the yielding flesh. Tassy slapped his hand away. Her molester responded by slapping her across the face. He yanked the robe from her shoulders and let it drop. The rapist grabbed her bloomers, whipped them down her legs, and yanked them over her feet. Tassy gasped. Her heart pounded all the more, and her body trembled with dread. The man pulled off his jacket. His chest swelled beneath his black t-shirt. Unbuckling his belt, the attacker jerked his pants and boxers down past his knees.

Then he dove on top of his victim, grasping her wrists and holding them down, compressing his weight against her body. Tassy snarled between clinched teeth. She clamped her eyes shut in protest, wheezing as she fought for air. Panting, the man's smelly breath blew into her face. It reeked of liquor. A sinister chuckle reached her ears. Tassy knew that it emanated from the boy called "Reg".

She felt her molester pressing against her loins. She felt his member grow rigid.

Then he thrust deep and hard into her. It felt like a knife being thrust into her heart. With a shriek, Tassy arched against him. Tears streamed down her cheeks, as she sobbed. The man's violent thrusting seemed unending. How could an act that had brought her such joy in the past be so abhorrent and terrible? How could an act that had thrilled her senses and provided such physical pleasure become painful, abrasive, and dreadful?

His stinking breath assailed her nostrils, as the rapist hissed, "Come on, bitch, you like it, and you know it! You never had a white man before, have you—a real man?"

His thrusts became more rapid and forceful. He pommeled her pelvis. Then there was one last push that drove her head against the headboard. With eyes clamped, Tassy whimpered. Her molester rose and climbed off of the bed. Drawing up her knees, the woman flopped over onto her side and, immersed in her misery, faced the wall.

But her plight wasn't over. She felt another body mount the bed. Grabbing a handful of hair, Reggie gave a yank. With a cry, Tassy rose to her hands and knees. And, from behind, the brunette plunged into her. Still clutching her hair, Reg pulled back her head. To keep his ardent thrusts from driving her face into the wall, the victim braced her palms against it. The rapist slapped her on the hips. He grunted and yelped, as if he were a rowdy cowhand riding a spirited bronc. As did the blonde, Reg finished with a final forceful thrust. For a moment, he knelt behind her, panting. While the molester moved from the bed, Tassy remained on her hands and knees, gasping and burying her head against the mattress. She began to convulse with sobs.

"Okay, Arvy," Reggie addressed the third member, of the trio, "your turn."

In despair, the victim shook her head against the mattress.

But the other boy groaned. "No. I just wanna get outta here."

The other two began taunting him.

"Ah, come on, Arvy! Can't you get it up?"

"You too good to do a nigger?"

"She's nice and tight, isn't she, Reg?"

"Hell yeah!"

Arvy sullenly responded, "I'm goin'."

Tassy sensed their departure, as the ribbing remarks faded.

"You should'a had a drink, Arvy; that would'a loosened you up."

"Yeah, you gotta stop bein' a wet blanket."

"Hey, the pickaninny is gettin' up. You wanna give 'im one last smack?"

"Hey, kid, you alright? Let me help you."

Tassy heard the impact of a blow, a hissing moan, muted chuckles, then silence.

Zadok stood over his son.

"Giddy," he whispered, "Gideon, can you hear me?"

The boy didn't respond but lay, with his eyes closed, breathing slow and deep. Zadok assumed that the doctor had given him something more for pain. With a despairing sigh, the man ambled across the room and stood at the window, staring out into the night. His thoughts on his family, Zadok began to reminisce.

He recalled the first time he had seen his wife. At the time, she was Tarissa Berry, age sixteen, and she was standing in the churchyard with her parents. The lacy white dress that she wore complimented her ginger brown skin. Tassy had the face of an angel: dark almond eyes, high cheek bones, a button nose and full shapely lips. Her delicate round chin and tapered jawline gave her face a heart shape. White ribbons contrasted with her raven black hair, draping over her high broad shoulders in wavy curls. She looked taller than she actually stood. Her figure was slim and shapely: small firm breasts, a tapering torso. Her narrow waist gave way to high round hips and long shapely legs.

That day, the twenty-four-year-old Zadok began devising his plans to court and eventually marry the angelic beauty. An independent manual laborer, the young man began taking on extra work, laboring almost every day, from daybreak to dusk. He had no trouble finding work, for he had long ago established a good reputation for himself. And he would only hire out to men whom he knew he could trust to be fair.

Although he supported his widowed mother as well as himself, the young man managed to save money. Over time, he bought building materials and erected a house near Josiah Black's wooded property. Zadok had done a lot of work for Josiah, and the landowner liked the young man, so Josiah sold the laborer the lot at a bargain price. During the construction, Zadok's mother moved in with a white family up North, where she served as a nanny and tutor.

Nearly two years had passed since he had first seen Tassy, and Zadok had completed the simple but sound house. And he was ready to introduce himself to the Berry family. He felt Mr. and Mrs. Berry's approval right away; his reputation as a hard worker and an honorable man had preceded him. And Zadok had developed an impressive bearing. His confidence and determination showed in his handsome face and erect posture. And he offset his dignified demeanor, which might have been considered "uppity" with a deference towards his "betters", yet without demeaning himself. He was considerate and solicitous towards the girl's parents. And he doted on Tassy as well.

At eighteen, she had become even more beautiful, having developed a sophisticated maturity. Four months after Zadok began courting Tassy, the two were married.

With a heavy sigh, the man turned from the window and, once more, stationed himself over his sleeping son. He recalled that after seven years of marriage, the couple resigned themselves to being childless. Zadok didn't care. He married Tassy not because he wanted someone to bear him children or to keep house for him, but because he loved her. And nothing else mattered. He tried to convince his wife of that.

Yet, when Tassy discovered that she was with child, Zadok was nearly as elated, as was his wife. The day Gideon was born, his mother had a hard labor, but without complications. His son emerged with his little face scrunched in a sour scowl. Eyes squinting and mouth gaping, the baby cried. After the midwife had cut the umbilical cord and swaddled the child, she handed him to his father. Zadok gazed down on the wrinkled face and thought of how homely his son appeared.

He smiled at the memory. Once Gideon had nursed and had fallen asleep, nuzzling at his mother's breast, Zadok's assessment had changed. The calm sleeping babe was adorable. And the boy grew more handsome each day. Twelve years later, Gideon was a tall good-looking boy. And here he lay, beaten.

Frowning, Zadok questioned why this had to happen. Why did God allow this to happen to his family? Where were their so-called guardian angels? He recalled hearing a fellow giving God credit for something as trivial as leading him to his favorite fishing hole after getting lost. No angels came to his family's aid when they were being brutalized. Maybe colored folk didn't have guardian angels. Zadok recalled hearing someone say that Christianity was a white man's religion. And some believed that Negroes didn't even have souls.

Maybe God didn't care about the colored folk; maybe he had turned his back on them. Maybe he did see them as inferior and unworthy of his attention. Maybe the Negroes' adoption of Christianity was a futile progression, a hopeless attempt to better one's self, to improve one's lot in life, or to merely cling to the hope of a better afterlife. After all, he reasoned, look how coloreds were beaten, lynched, burned—and raped. And yet, most of them were good, gentle, humble folk. Zadok knew that most of the retribution suffered by the coloreds at the hands of whites was unjustified. What Negro, in his right mind, would have the nerve to commit such offenses of which they were being accused?

Of course, many of the offenses for which coloreds were tortured or killed were trivial, insignificant. Zadok recalled the case of fourteen-year-old Emmett Till. The boy, having come from Chicago, was visiting his great uncle in Mississippi. He and some other boys had gathered in town. On a dare, Emmett entered a grocery store and, on his way out, said to the white woman behind the counter, "Bye, babe!" For that offense, the young boy was picked up in the middle of the night, from his uncle's place, by the clerk's husband and half-brother.

A few days later, a fisherman found the boy's naked and battered body in the Tallahatchie River. Zadok had heard how Emmett's body was bloated and his face distorted. The disturbing thought sent chills through him. That had happened only a few years ago. The father shivered at the idea that something like that could happen to his son. He amended, in his mind, that an awful abuse had been visited on his son.

The two men who had abducted Emmett Till were found innocent. In other words, they were justified, because a young colored boy got "uppity" and insulted his "betters". Disgusted by the thought, Zadok lowered his head.

That's what they called colored people who wanted to be treated with dignity, "uppity". And he knew many folk considered him "uppity". He didn't shuffle about with his shoulders slumped and his head bowed. When spoken to by white and colored alike, the man looked the speaker in the eye. He lived better than other Negroes in the area, though it was a modest existence by general standards. And many whites hated him for it, though he never had any trouble—until now.

His teeth clenched, Zadok raised his doubled fist and wanted to slam it into something. His fury was like a river surging against a dam.

The man heard the creaking of the door and turned to face Dr. Orley. Zadok caught the startled look in the doctor's gray eyes. Realizing that his expression must have looked fierce, the black man relaxed his body. Dr. Orley seemed to do the same. And Zadok reminded himself that there were other white folk, like the doctor, who showed kindness and respect to the colored people.

Hanging his head, the physician removed his glasses and wiped the lenses. "Well," he reluctantly began, "you probably can guess what happened." He met Zadok's anxious eyes. "She was raped."

The affirmation of his fears sent chills charging through the husband's body, and his broad frame trembled. His heart pounded. His eyes welled with tears.

"I suspected," the brooding man muttered, "but I didn't know for sure." He shook his bowed head. "I didn't want to know." Silently, he stared into space.

The doctor sighed. Then he related all that Tassy had told him about the terrible ordeal. Tears trickled down Zadok's face, reaching his clenched jaw. Rage churned and mingled with agony.

Concluding the details, Dr. Orley shook his bowed head. "Zadok, this just makes me sick, that somebody could—I-I'm real sorry."

Nostrils flared, the black man gave a stiff nod then looked away. The two stood in silence.

Then, the doctor spoke, "I've got an extra cot I can roll out here for you."

"No thanks, doc," Zadok replied in a heavy voice. "I'll just sit up, in a chair. I can't sleep tonight."

Dr. Orley laid his hand on the black man's shoulder. "Again, I'm real sorry. But they should sleep well, through the night. I gave them each something to relieve the pain and the stress."

The physician patted the broad shoulder and forced a weak smile beneath his silver mustache. "It will be better tomorrow."

Then he left the room.

Zadok walked over to the adjacent room, where his wife lay sleeping on the padded table. The cover draping her body gently rose and fell with the rhythm of her breaths. He looked on her bruised but calm face. Tassy was beautiful, gentle, and loving. It was so wrong for her to have been abused so.

He noticed his wife's undergarments draped over the back of the chair. And he suddenly realized that she would need proper clothing for the following day. It wouldn't hurt to bring fresh clothing for Gideon as well. So he left the doctor's house and climbed into his pickup.

Zadok tried to focus his mind on the twinkling stars dappling the clear black sky. But his thoughts turned to his wife's account of the attack, as relayed by Dr. Orley. She hadn't recognized the boys. They may have been from out of town. She had mentioned three names: Reg, Arvy and Bernie. It wasn't much to go on, but somehow he would find out who were those boys, the brutes who assaulted his family. They would pay.

His family's suffering would not be dismissed, as of no account. Their feelings were significant; they mattered. And there would be justice, even if he had to dispense it out himself. He would avenge them. And the thought somewhat relieved his troubled mind.

Zadok's thoughts of justice and vengeance persisted for the entire drive to his home. Halting the truck in front of the house, he started across the yard when his eyes fell on the carcass of the family dog.

He walked over and looked down on the lifeless creature, murmuring, "Poor Duke. Guess I ought to take care of you."

The man skirted the front porch to the other side of the house and strode to the garage. Zadok could hear the drone of the generator that was enclosed in a small shed behind the car shed. Hinges squeaking, the man entered pitch darkness when he opened the side door. Zadok entered into the dark. His eyes barely adjusted, but he knew where the shovel stood. Spade in hand, Zadok left the garage and walked to the back of the house. He crossed the sparse lawn and halted near the weathered pole-corral that penned a Holstein heifer and her cross-bred black calf.

A few paces from the cow shed, the man began digging. It wasn't long before he had dug an adequate hole. Then Zadok collected the carcass and gently laid the family dog in the grave. Gazing down on the creature, one last time, he eulogized, "You were a good ol' dog, Duke, Giddy's best friend. This will probably hurt him more than the beating he took."

He sighed. "Well..."

The man began covering the carcass with the dark dirt. After returning the shovel to the garage, Zadok entered the house. The front room was still lit with soft light. Hands on hips, he looked over the strewn furniture and decided to take the time to put things in place. While straightening the room, the man made his way to the table abutting the wall. There, Mrs. Baird's strawberry-rhubarb pies sat. Zadok smiled. As if on cue, his stomach growled. Taking the pies, he placed them in the refrigerator.

When he finished the housework, the man went to the bedroom that he and his wife shared. He took from the closet a blue dress spangled with a white floral design. Collecting fresh underwear for his wife, Zadok remembered to grab her black slip-on shoes. Then, he halted. Here was where he found his family, his wife kneeling in her torn camisole, stooped over in sorrow and shame, and his son, lying on the bed, weak and aching.

The covers were rumpled. The pillow laid on the floor. Here was where his wife was ravaged. The man's broad shoulders slumped. Lost in a wash of melancholy, he vacantly stared down on the bed. When he finally pulled himself out of the gloom, Zadok decided to strip the bedding. At least his family could come home to a clean orderly house. And he hoped that would be some consolation. The man smirked at the thought as he whipped the bedding from the mattress.

He found some relief in doing the chores. They were a beneficial distraction. When Zadok finished hanging the washed bedding over the clotheslines, he decided to clean up himself as well, and showered. The hot water was soothing as it spattered against his aching muscles. For a moment, he freed his mind of the dreadful thoughts. His mind and senses basked in the refreshing hot water. When the water began to cool, the man turned off the shower.

Drying himself and dressing, Zadok gathered his family's clothing, climbed into his pickup, and headed back to town.

The feelings of anger and anguish seemed to recede back into his mind, still there, but vague, like the distant sounds of chirping crickets and the croaking toads on a warm quiet evening. His commitment for vengeance was also vague, yet there.

As Zadok drove through town, the clock in front of the town hall showed that it was nearly four in the morning. The man pulled into Dr. Orley's driveway, entered the house, and went to the room where his son rested. Seeing Gideon lying there added potency to the dreary emotions that had been dormant. But Zadok was weary. He pulled up a chair next to the cot, and sat there, resting his chin on his fist. His mind became addled and seemed to blank. He finally drifted off, into an exhausted sleep.

Gideon woke up to aching pain throughout his torso, and his face throbbed. He opened his eyes to the sight of a white ceiling. The boy was disoriented and confused. As he looked about, Gideon found his father sitting next to him, asleep, his stacked hands providing a crude pillow for his cheek.

"Pop," the boy's faint voice rasped.

Zadok raised his head, his lids drooping over red eyes.

Sucking a deep breath through his nose, the man stiffly pulled back his shoulders. "Yes, son?"

"Where am I?"

"Doc Orley's place."

With a wince, the man arched and shifted his back from side to side. "How do you feel, son?"

It was Gideon's turn to wince, as he shifted his body and braced himself on his elbows. "I'm stiff and sore."

His father forced a smile. "Well, you—you took quite a beating. Do you remember what happened?"

Furrowing his brow, the boy answered, "Yeah. Three white boys came into our house. They just walked in." He paused a moment. "They acted funny and smelled. They were loud too." A pang shot through his side when Gideon shifted to face his father. "I asked them what they wanted. This big fella shoved me against the table. I told them to get out, and they just laughed. They were headed into the kitchen. And I went over to the stove and grabbed a chunk of wood. They laughed at me again. But I started swinging."

A smile stretched across the boy's face. "I whacked the big fella in the knee and nicked him in the ribs! He went back into one of the chairs! Then another boy came at me. I kept swinging at him and caught him on the arm! I got him pretty good!"

Gideon noticed the pride in his father's smiling eyes. Then, the boy's smile faded. "But then he got the best of me; he beat me up."

And the delight in Zadok's eyes was replaced with regret.

Suddenly, Gideon started. "Is Mama okay?"

His father's eyes welled and glistened. "She was hurt too, son. But Doc Orley tended to her." Zadok forced a weak smile across his somber face. "She's resting in the other room."

His son stared into space. "I remember one of the boys saying something about how pretty she was." With concern, he met his father's eyes. "Did they hurt her bad?"

Zadok dropped his gaze. "Well, ah—I don't—I..." Tears started from the man's eyes and trickled down his cheeks.

Tolerating the pain, Gideon sat up. He felt his own tears running down his face. "Pop, I tried; I really did try." Gideon brushed his tears away, before his father cupped the back of his neck with a large hand.

"I know, son."

They sat in a silent, sullen reverie.

"Pop," the boy broke the quiet. "I remember a picture on the back of the big fella's jacket. It was a red razorback." He stared at the wall. "That just sticks in my mind—a mean-looking razor-back. It was the last thing I'd seen when they walked out the door."

Dr. Orley entered the room.

"Oh good!" The doctor perked. "You're awake! How are you feeling this morning, Giddy?"

"Good morning, sir." With a faint smile, the boy greeted the doctor. "I'm stiff and sore."

"It's no wonder." The physician stood before Gideon and cupped his chin, raising the boy's head and assessing his visage. "I'll give you a couple more pain killers right now and give some to your daddy to take home for later."

Placing the white tablets in Gideon's hand, Dr. Orley fetched a glass of water and handed it to his patient.

As the boy swallowed the pills, the doctor stated, "You'll probably be sore for several days, but it will get better. There are no broken bones." Smiling, he vigorously rubbed Gideon's head. "You're young and tough. You're a brave boy."

Dr. Orley turned to Zadok. "I've got patients to see. You can take your family home, but take your time."

He glanced at the fresh clothing in the black man's lap. "I see you brought clean clothes from home. If Tassy is up to it, she may want to bathe before putting those on."

Turning to the boy, the physician pointed a long finger at him. "You can wash up too; you smell!"

The two grinned at one another.

As Zadok stood and lay the clothing on the seat of the chair, he stretched his back muscles. Then Dr. Orley handed him a bottle of medication. The physician placed his hand on the black man's shoulder and squeezed. "Have them take two tablets every four hours or so. I'll look in on Tassy before I tend to my other patients"

Zadok nodded.

As the doctor retreated to the adjacent room, the father gathered up his son's fresh clothes. "You feel up to a bath?"

"Yep."

Gideon gingerly slid off of the table. His legs shook.

"Are you going to be okay?" Zadok asked.

"Yes."

Gideon took the clothes from his father and staggered a few steps, but recovered, and made his way to the entry. There, with a questioning look, he turned to Zadok.

His father told him, "Take a left and go down the hall. It will be on your right."

With a smile and a nod, Gideon left the room and made his way down the hall to the bathroom. The boy ran the water into the enamel tub. As he pulled off his clothes, Gideon winced at the twinges of pain. It felt good to sink into the hot water. Turning off the spigot as the level neared the lip of the tub, Gideon basked in the soothing wet heat.

The bath eased his body but not his mind. The boy brooded as he soaked. He felt ashamed for failing his mother, for letting his father down. While his father was away, working, Gideon was acting man of the house. But when the brutes invaded his home, he wasn't man enough to drive them off. He lacked the strength and the power. Maybe he was lacking in courage and determination as well. He had been beaten, subdued, defeated. The boy huddled, like a weakling, as the intruders descended on his mother and hurt her.

A tear wended down the boy's cheek.

Zadok could hear the doctor's voice emanating from the next room, but he couldn't make out what the man was saying.

Finally, Dr. Orley came out and approached him. "I gave her medication." For a moment, the physician seemed to ponder. Then, taking hold of the black man's arm, Dr. Orley leaned towards Zadok and, just above a whisper, murmured, "This...sort of trauma affects different women in different ways. I mean some handle it better than do others, and some are just overcome by it. Whatever the degree of difficulty, the woman typically feels guilty and ashamed..."

Glowering, Zadok interjected, "Guilty! Why on earth should Tassy feel guilty?"

"She shouldn't. But something about this trauma causes people to think and act irrationally." With a shrug, the physician continued, "A woman might think that she had done something to provoke the attack; maybe she happened to look a certain way or acted a certain way. Sometimes, the people around her might cause her to feel guilty by what they say or do."

Zadok furrowed his brow. "Well, I know that Tassy is guilty of nothing. She was raped because she was a lowly colored woman. And that isn't her fault." He looked away. "That was God's doing."

Laying his hand, on the black man's shoulder, the doctor replied, "I know she's not guilty. It's just that a terrible experience like this really damages a woman, emotionally and mentally. Her feelings may confuse her. She may blame herself. She may blame you. Who knows?"

"Those boys are the ones at fault!" the black man snarled, his eyes smoldering.

"I know," the physician sighed. "I know."

After a silent pause, Dr. Orley tugged at his collar. "Well, I'd better tend to my other patients." At the doorway, he turned. "Look, it will be difficult for Tassy to go home, after..."

"I've decide to take her to my mother's house," Zadok muttered.

Dr. Orley nodded. "Good, good." Hesitating for an awkward moment, the doctor then stepped out into the hall.

The door to the adjacent room creaked. Turning, Zadok found his wife stepping out with a beige blanket wrapped about her body. Her dull eyes seemed hollow, her mouth set in a forlorn frown. The woman looked like someone who had just lost everything she had ever had in the world, like someone cast into a void.

As she slowly walked into the room, Zadok approached. He gently wrapped his arms around his wife and held her. He felt her body spasm with silent sobs. The man pressed his lips to the crown of her head.

When he finally let her go, Tassy stumbled over to the chair beside the examining table, and collapsed into the seat. Her high cheeks glistened with spent tears. Zadok stood beside her, caressing her shoulders, while she stared down at the wood floor.

After a time of sullen quiet, Gideon, donned in a fresh plaid shirt and denim jeans, entered the room. A smile spread over his face as he looked upon his mother and father. But his smile disappeared as abruptly as it had surfaced. He walked over to his parents. Looking upon her son, Tassy rose to her feet.

As they embraced, Gideon apologized. "I'm sorry, Mama!"

"Oh, my poor boy." His mother lamented, nestling her chin in the crook of his neck. She let out the last of her tears.

Zadok gathered up her garments from the chair and waited until his wife and son parted. Then he led Tassy down the hall to the bathroom. The man turned on the water.

Sitting on the edge of the tub, Zadok looked up into his wife's glum face. "Tassy, I love you more than anything in the whole wide world, and nothing will ever change that."

Only for a moment did her lowered gaze meet his. Rising, her husband laid the clothes on top of a nearby hamper and embraced Tassy, before rejoining his son in the examining room.

There, his son faced him and, once again, apologized. "I'm sorry, Pop."

Zadok placed his arm around the boy's shoulders. "Son, you did the best that you could. You tried to protect your mama, and you took a beating for it. But you stepped up, and you tried. You have nothing to be sorry for, boy. You did good, and I'm proud of you."

Despite the praise, Gideon hung his head. His father embraced him.

The two waited quietly together, each lost in his own morose thoughts, until Tassy returned to the room. Zadok felt his cheeks warm at the sight of her. The blue and white dress complimented her golden skin. Despite her dark hollow eyes and glum expression, his wife was yet beautiful. He wanted to rush over to her, wrap the woman in his arms, and smother her with kisses. But instead, Zadok calmly approached and laid an arm about her shoulders.

"Tassy," he explained, "I'm going to take you and Giddy to my mother's house."

His wife nodded.

She then looked up to her son and sadly smiled. "Are you alright, Giddy?"

The boy walked over to his parents. "I'm alright, Mama. And you?"

Responding with brief rapid nods, Tassy answered, "I'll be alright."

The three embraced and held one another. Then Zadok led his family through the hallway. As they passed the parlor, Dr. Orley spied them through the entry while he knelt beside a young black girl and her mother. The physician acknowledged them with a slight nod. And Zadok responded in kind.

The family emerged into the bright warm morning sun. But the pleasant day did little, if anything, to alleviate the melancholy that permeated the family. They entered the cab. Tassy sat between her husband and son. As they rode through town, Zadok held his wife's hand. The woman stared out through the windshield as if in a trance, just as she had the night before. Concerned, her husband wondered how long she would be like this—hopefully, not for the rest of her life. The words she had spoken earlier, "I'll be alright," were encouraging, but it was easier said than done. Perhaps, the damage would diminish with time. But Zadok suspected there would always be a remnant of the injury there, sorrow, shame, and fear.

Distracted as he was, the man was only subconsciously aware of the flowing countryside: Canby's dairy, Packard's mule farm, Henshaw's peas and green beans, Sample's hog farm, Anderson's cotton field, Kendall's beef cattle, Pettyjohn's cornfield, Tibbideau's sweet potato patch and Black's woods.

Time and space passed unnoticed. Zadok was submerged into another dimension. But when he came to the turn off leading to his property, the man returned to the real world. Climbing the dirt road, he pulled the truck into his yard and shut off the engine.

Suddenly, it dawned on him.

He turned to his son, who stared out of the passenger window, and reluctantly informed him that his dog, Duke, was dead. Both Tassy and Gideon gawked at the man. A tear started from the woman's reddened eye. The boy turned away, with a bleak sigh, and slumped in the seat.

Zadok began to climb out of the cab, when his son asked, "Pop, where is he?"

"I buried him near the cow shed."

Tassy patted Gideon's shoulder. Stepping from the truck, the boy plodded to the back yard as though he had been trudging for miles. The man felt for his son. It wasn't enough that he had been beaten and his mother brutalized, but Gideon had also lost his best friend. And with all of that, they were about to leave the only home the boy ever knew, perhaps for good. A gloomy essence haunted the place now.

Leaning through the cab door, Zadok addressed his wife, "You can stay here, if you want, Tassy."

With a deep breath, the woman shook her head. She slid across the seat, and her husband took her hand. As they climbed the porch, the woman's grip tightened. She gasped when Zadok opened the door. Crossing the threshold, Tassy froze. With concern, Zadok studied her.

He released her hand and, making his way across the front room, asked, "Is there anything, in particular that you want to take along?"

The woman shook her head. Zadok plodded to their bedroom. He took a worn brown suitcase from the closet and carefully folded some dresses, laying them within. While he gathered underclothes and personal items for his wife, Zadok glanced through the bedroom window and saw his son kneeling beside Duke's grave. Knitting his brows, the father pursed his lips, aching for the boy.

He went out of the back door and crossed the yard to where Gideon knelt, and placed his hand on the boy's shoulder.

"I'm really sorry, son."

"Yeah," Gideon wiped a tear, from his cheek, "he was a good ol' dog."

"Yes, he was," the father agreed. "Maybe we can get another dog sometime."

His son shrugged. Patting the boy's shoulder, Zadok suggested, "Why don't you pack, and we'll head to Grandma's?"

It was late afternoon when the faded blue GMC pulled up in front of a white-trimmed slate gray house. Gideon leaped out of the cab and gathered the suitcase and his bundle from the truck bed. Then he dashed through the gate of the white picket fence and over the walk leading to the porch. As Tassy climbed out of the cab, Zadok took her hand.

Blue hyacinths, red dahlias, yellow daffodils, and white garde-
nias, flourishing from the flower boxes bordering the foundation,
festooned the front of the house. A cherry tree stretched towards
the sun from one side of the rich green yard, while a beech tree
towered over the other side. Zadok felt his spirit somewhat up-
lifted. He was eager to see his mother. He had been busy of late,
and more than a month had passed since his family's last visit.

Though his hands were full, Gideon managed to rap on the
door and turn the knob. His parents followed him into the house.

"Mama!" Zadok called out.

The woman emerged from the kitchen, wiping her hands on
her apron. Her gray hair was rolled into a bun. With age, her
weight had settled, and the once slim figure of her youth had
grown slightly plump. Yet, she remained an attractive woman.
Her eyes glinted with delight behind her wire-rimmed glasses,
and a white smile beamed from her lovely brown face.

"Why, Zadok, what a pleasant surpri..." The woman's smile
fell as she gaped, her startled gaze turning from her son's weary
visage to Tassy's forlorn stare.

Her voice dropped an octave. "What's the matter, boy!"

"Let us get settled, Mama, and I'll tell you."

Gideon sat the suitcase beside the armrest of the sofa and
placed his bundle on a cushion. While the boy gave his grandmother a hug, Tassy drifted over to the upholstered armchair and
sat. Embracing her grandson, the old woman's eyes followed her
daughter-in-law. Then she frowned at her son. When they loosened their embrace, Gideon's grandmother looked into his face.
Then, with a scowl, she held his chin in her cupped hand and
raised his head. Again, she turned to Zadok.

The man led the way into the kitchen.

He quietly said, "I need to leave Tassy and Giddy here for a
few days."

His mother seemed to search his eyes with anticipation.

When Zadok failed to elaborate, he thought, like a roiling pot, she would boil over.

She spoke in a low growl, "I know you didn't lay a hand on your precious wife and son!" In a cadence, the woman pressed, "What is the matter, boy?"

He finally spoke. "You have some coffee, Mama?"

His mother lowered and shook her head. When she looked up, her eyes seemed to smolder. "Good lord, Zadok! Help yourself to the coffee! I'll heat some water for tea." Glaring at her son, she demanded in a forceful hiss, "But then you tell me what the hell is the matter! You hear me?"

Chastened, Zadok nodded. He couldn't recall a time when his mother swore. He poured a cup of coffee. While his mother put the kettle on the stove, the man leaned against the counter, gripping the edge with his free hand. The woman faced him with arms folded. Her mouth was pinched in a tight frown.

Staring down at the tile floor, Zadok muttered, "Mama, Tassy was raped."

He heard his mother gasp and looked up to find her hand covering her gaping mouth.

"Zadok!" she wheezed.

The man fidgeted while he gave his mother a general account of the horrid ordeal. He watched her face contort with emotion. Tears welled up in her large dark eyes.

Zadok concluded, "I need to leave Tassy and Giddy here for a few days. I've got things to take care of back home."

His mother's furrowed brow deepened. "What are you planning to do, boy?"

Looking away, Zadok shuffled his feet.

"Zadok!" She prodded.

The man turned to the demanding woman. "I don't know, Mama; I'm not sure yet."

Once more pursing her lips, she thrust her fists onto her wide hips. Zadok glanced through the archway into the living room. The tea kettle began to whistle. He watched his mother prepare the tea for Tassy.

With a cup in hand, the woman turned and faced her son. She arched a brow. "I'm going to take Tassy upstairs. She probably needs to rest. Then you and I are going to have a talk!" She wagged a finger at him. "And you are not going to be evasive!"

Looking into his coffee, Zadok conceded, "Yes, ma'am."

When his mother left the kitchen, the man turned and gazed out of the window and spied his son sitting on the back porch swing, petting his grandmother's gray tabby. He stepped out of the back door. Joining the boy, Zadok sat next to Gideon and affectionately scrubbed his son's head.

The father sipped his coffee and looked into the evening sky. The sun was low and bright. The heat of the day began to wane. Closing his eyes, Zadok basked in the calm. He heard the leaves of the trees rattling in the gentle breeze. The scents of persimmon and lilac reached his nostrils. The man opened his eyes and peered into the backyards of the surrounding homes. They were empty and quiet.

For a moment, Zadok let his troubles fall away. For a moment, all that existed were the elm and persimmon trees, the lilacs, and the sounds of magpies calling to one another from their perches. For a moment, he was transported into a Garden of Eden.

Then his thoughts turned to his wife. The man became burdened with a sense of guilt; he had failed her. And, though it would not eradicate the terrible wounds she has suffered, Zadok would vindicate her, somehow.

He couldn't remain seated. The man could hardly stand being still and wished he could run away from himself. Of course, he couldn't. But just the same, the restless husband rose and walked back into the house. He entered the kitchen. Draining his coffee cup, Zadok refilled it and, once again, leaned against the counter.

His mother returned to the kitchen and, scowling, confronted him. "Tassy's lying down. I tried to talk to her, but all she would say is, 'They hurt me. They hurt me.'" The woman shook her bowed head. "That poor girl. And Giddy..."

Looking up, Zadok's mother fixed her hardened eyes on her son and folded her arms over her breasts. "So, what is it that you are planning to do, boy?"

Zadok took a deep breath and reluctantly answered, "I'm going to find those boys who did this. Then, I don't know what I'm going to do. But I know what I want to do!"

The woman narrowed her eyes. "Look, boy, that won't undo what happened. All you will end up doing is getting yourself in trouble—or killed, like your father!"

There was a silence, as Zadok recalled what had happened to his father. Zebulon Quarry had been working with a gang of black laborers, who were clearing land for a property owner. When the employer cheated them on their pay, Zadok's father spoke to the owner, who agreed to make restitution. But their employer continued cheating the men. So Zebulon instructed the crew to abandon the work. Soon afterwards, Zadok's father was returning home from another job he had taken, and on the road, he was shot from the back of his mule and killed.

"You weren't quite Gideon's age when that happened," his mother reminded him. "And the suffering was financial as well as emotional. Don't do that to your family, son. They need you."

Scowling, the man hissed, through clenched teeth, "I've got to, Mama! To do nothing would-would eat at my soul! It would be admitting, that my family is of no account—just niggers, who were used by their betters! It would be admitting that their pain and suffering amounted to nothing! They don't matter! I have to show different! I have to react, because they do matter! And if I don't do something about it," he let out a sigh, "you know nobody else will."

His mother rebutted, "You are going to do this for yourself, not your family! You are going to do this in order to expel the rage and anger—and your guilt! You are going to do this so you can feel better about yourself!"

Wearily, Zadok sighed, while the woman frowned at him. "Yes, Mama, I suppose I am going to do this for myself. But it is for my family too." Again, he hissed out a breath. "Mama, if I don't do anything, I won't be able to live with myself. I'll-I'll end up a broken defeated man, like those colored men in Darky Town, hollow-eyed, with their faces in the dirt. That is no way for a man to live, colored or otherwise. And if I did end up like that, how would my family live with it? I would bring them down into the dirt with me."

There was silence.

Then, his mother responded, "So go off and get yourself killed! Then they can end up in the dirt by themselves! Zadok, you are yet a strong man. You can go on providing for your family. You can yet be an example for your boy and encourage him. You can yet be a comfort to your wife and cherish her. 'It is better to be a live coward, than a dead hero.'"

The man peered into his mother's grave visage. "I don't want to live if I have to live as a coward! If I can't look into my son's eyes without feeling shame, if I can't hold my wife in my arms and feel deserving of her love and respect, then I'd rather be dead."

His nostrils flared as he glowered. "And I'm glad Papa was the way he was and died for it, rather than ending up with no self-worth, rotting away in Darky Town, or in some shanty." He turned his smoldering eyes away. "Papa gave me pride and dignity in the twelve years that I had him. That's better than a lifetime of shame and self-loathing."

Once more, Zadok looked into his mother's eyes. "Mama, would you bring Papa back if you could, and change him from the man he was? Would you have him here with us, wasting away, hating who he was and regretting what he couldn't do for his family?

"Yes, when Papa died, it was a struggle; we both had to work hard. But we did it. I succeeded because of who Papa was, and because of what he taught me. And it's fearful to think how I might have turned out had Papa backed down and groveled. And if I have to..."

The man went silent when Gideon walked through the kitchen door. Zadok put his arm around his son. They smiled as they looked to one another.

"Mama," the father began, "do you have any lemonade in the fridge?"

Wearily, the woman answered. "Yes."

Zadok squeezed his son. "Want some?"

"Yes, sir!"

Reaching into the cupboard, the man asked the woman, "Want some, Mama?"

With a grimace, the woman scolded, "'Would you like some'! Didn't I teach you better, than that? I was a teacher, for God's sake!"

Wide-eyed, Gideon gawked up at his father. Never had he heard his grandmother speak in such a way, skirting blasphemy like that. Zadok dismissed it with a wrinkle of his nose and a brief shake of his head. Then he took three glasses from the cupboard. His son had taken the pitcher of lemonade from the refrigerator and filled the glasses. Gideon handed his grandmother and his father each a glass.

As Gideon took a drink, Zadok laid a hand on the boy's shoulder.

"You took quite a beating last night," the man stated, looking over to his mother.

"Yeah," Gideon grunted between gulps.

"It didn't help your mama though, did it?"

Dispirited, the boy cast down his gaze and moaned. "No."

Zadok caught the look of reproof in his mother's scowling visage.

But he pressed on. "If you had it to do over again, knowing that your mother would still be hurt, knowing that you couldn't stop those men, would you still fight back and take the beating?"

Wide-eyed, Gideon exclaimed, "Yeah!"

His father grinned with pride. Then, Zadok asked, "Why?"

Pondering the question, the boy frowned. Then he stated, "Because I would have to do something! I would at least have to try!"

"Even if you knew it wouldn't change anything?"

"Well, yeah! I-I would just have to!" He looked up into his father's eyes. "Wouldn't you, Pop?"

"Damn right!"

Suppressing a vindicated grin, Zadok looked over to his mother.

Her scowl remaining, the woman groused. "Zadok Quarry, you watch your language in my house! I'll take a switch to you, and don't think that I won't! I don't care how big and stubborn you are! And there is a big difference between a beating and getting killed!"

In confusion, Gideon wrinkled his nose as he looked up to his father.

The fuming woman turned away. "I have to make supper. The two of you get out of my kitchen!"

"We can help, Mama," Zadok offered.

"I don't need your help!" she barked, her back to the two. "Just go!"

The man led his baffled son into the living room.

Gideon murmured. "What's wrong with Grandma?"

"She's just upset about what happened to you and your mother." As his son took a seat on the sofa, Zadok asked, "You want to watch television, while supper is cooking?"

"Sure!" The boy beamed.

Tassy awoke to the aroma of cooking chicken. But it was the nightmare that had aroused her from sleep. The woman's moist eyes gaped at the ceiling, and she felt a chill, as beads of perspiration, covering her face and arms, cooled her warm skin.

It was bad enough that Tassy had actually suffered the rape, but now she was haunted by reliving it. And although the visions were surreal, in her dream state, they seemed real enough. In her subconscious mind, the woman found herself in her underwear standing outside of her bedroom door and peering into the living room, where she saw a huge brute facing her son and the leaping, yelping family dog. The brute looked like a character from a fairy tale book, a large bulky ogre. The character was donned in a tan tunic, covered by a black furry jerkin. His mussed hair was tawny. And Tassy recognized the distorted image to be that of the leader of the trio that had invaded her home, one of the two who had raped her.

Her son appeared small and young in her dream, perhaps about five years old. And, before the towering ogre, Gideon stood with a small branch in his hand.

There was a tall, thin, evil-looking creature standing next to the ogre. He had the visage of a goblin: big sharp ears, a long crooked nose, sharp teeth, and bushy black brows hooding evil eyes. His black hair was wild and unruly. His striped clothing resembled that of a convict's attire.

Another character looked normal and nonthreatening. But he was small in the dream, smaller than was Gideon. He stood back in a corner.

The ogre snatched up her son in an oversized hand, lifted the boy to his gaping mouth, and bit a chunk out of the child's belly.

Gideon let out a silent wail. The dog whined and scampered out of the open front door. Tassy felt a dreaded panic rise up inside of her. She let out a scream, yet no sound emitted from her throat. Even so, the eyes of the alerted intruders were drawn to her, and the big brute tossed the small body of her son out of the window.

Suddenly, Tassy realized that she was standing before them, naked; her garments had vanished. The ogre and goblin leered at her and advanced. The woman turned and fled into her room. She scampered to the side of the bed and, somehow, managed to slip underneath, where she sat with her knees tucked under her chin and her hands clasped about her legs. As ridiculous as was the imagery, she being able to fit, sitting upright under her bed, the vision seemed real enough in her unconscious mind.

Hiding under the bed in the dark, Tassy noticed the non-threatening miniature intruder standing under the foot of the bed, staring at her. He held his hands behind his back. The little fellow seemed misplaced. He appeared reluctant and glum. Though he was still and silent, Tassy sensed that he was somehow drawing the other two intruders to her.

Just as she suspected, the woman sensed the other two prowling near the bed. The edge of the bedspread was lifted, and the ugly ogre peered at her. With a gasp, Tassy scuttled from under the bed, passing the miniature intruder, and ran out of the back door into the night. A shift had suddenly enveloped her and flitted in the wind.

The woman spied her son, lying on his back, beside the house. Duke was licking and tugging on his entrails. Turning from the gory sight, Tassy fled to the chicken coop. She flung open the door and huddled, as she had under her bed, in a corner.

The woman heard the chickens clucking outside of the coop. Then she heard frantic squawking and the desperate flapping of wings. She saw the little intruder standing across from her, just as he had done under her bed. But then he walked through the wall and disappeared.

That was when Tassy woke up to the smell of cooking chicken. The irony would have amused her had the dream not mocked her actual tragedy.

With a deep sigh, the woman sat up on the bed. Her muscles were stiff and ached. The skin felt taut over her bruised cheek. Tassy stood and walked to the window. Outside, the sky was fading to an ever darkening blue. The foliage gently fluttered in a breeze. Only the whisper of the leaves and the chirping of crickets broke the evening quiet. Tassy felt misplaced in the tranquility, an alien, full of turmoil and discontent, haunted.

There was a knock, at the door.

Her mother-in-law entered. "Supper is almost ready, dear. You may want to wash up soon."

Her back to the old woman, Tassy silently nodded. Then her mother-in-law approached and, standing behind her, the old woman gently laid her hands on her daughter-in-law's shoulders. "You know, Tassy, that I couldn't love you any more than if you were my own flesh and blood. If there is anything I can do..."

Again, the young woman silently nodded. Her mother-in-law stood a brief moment longer, then walked away.

Tassy went into the bathroom and stood before the mirror. She frowned at the dark circles about her red eyes, her bruised cheek and her scabbed lip. The woman studied her pleasant features. She was still pretty. Tassy wasn't vain about her pleasing looks; it was just a fact, and she considered it a blessing from God. She was modestly flattered by other people's admiring looks and compliments, by her husband's loving gaze and praise.

But now, the woman felt tainted, filthy, unworthy of her husband, unworthy to be his wife, to be Gideon's mother. Tassy felt undeserving of anyone's admiration or approval. Why did she deserve to suffer her recent plight? Was she vain? Was God punishing her? Perhaps, to simply acknowledge that she was beautiful was wrong. What did the boy say, when he grabbed her? "Bernie was right, you ain't bad lookin', for a coon"?

Her life had once been wonderful. Even as a child, she was blessed. Tassy's father was a Baptist preacher, her mother an artist. They were well respected in their community by black folk and white alike. By colored standards, the family lived well and never wanted. Her parents were devout Christians and loving gentle people. She had always been happy.

Then Zadok Quarry came into her life, and her world became even more blissful. Whenever she was with that man, Tassy's being was filled with elation. And in his absence, she reveled in dreaming of him. The woman had entered ecstasy when he proposed to her, a bliss that was only surpassed by their marriage and wedding night. When Zadok made love to her, the union of body and soul brought the greatest joy, a euphoric delight. Such joy was only equaled by the birth of her son.

Perhaps, there was a price to pay for such good fortune. The night before, she paid that price. Her misery was equal to the pleasure she once had. What could be worse? But, as Tassy contemplated that question, a thought came to her: at least she still had her family, though she felt estranged from them now. Tassy was out of place. She no longer belonged in this family. But the woman would go through the motions and continue her role as mother and wife, because she needed them. The only thing worse than existing as a pariah among her own would be to have to go on without them.

Shaking her head, Tassy dismissed the overwhelming thoughts and washed her face and hands. Then she descended the stairs and joined her family at the supper table. She was self-conscious over their charitable smiles and gazes. Feeling awkward, the woman took her seat, catty-corner to her husband's position at the head of the table.

Zadok's mother asked him to say the blessing over the meal.

"Mama," he stammered, "I—ah...why don't you say the blessing?"

With a solemn nod of understanding, the old woman bowed her head and proceeded. "Our Father, we thank you for providing us with this good food. But, as you know, we have greater concerns and greater troubles. You know what tragedy this family has suffered, particularly our girl Tassy and our boy Gideon."

Tassy felt the heat flush her face. Why did the family have to dwell on the plight? She couldn't forget what had happened, but she didn't want others dwelling on it, as well.

"You know their pain and anguish," the old woman continued. "We ask for the strength, of your spirit, to best endure this hardship. The physical wounds will heal soon enough. But we need your special attention to endure the emotional afflictions, the breaking of the spirit. Help us, Lord, and guide us in the ways to help one another, through this trying time. You have the power, Father; you are the power. You can heal us. And we ask you to, in the name of your blessed son, Jesus Christ. Amen."

If only the Lord would, Tassy thought to herself. If only the memory of that night could be wiped away. But, would God do that for her, or did he want her to suffer? Time would tell. She had to hope that it would get better, that her despair would wane.

Zadok began dishing up servings of chicken and dumplings into bowls. His son ate with gusto. Tassy was pleased to see that, at least, Gideon seemed to be recovering from his abuse. She felt the eyes of her husband and mother-in-law on her from time to time as she twiddled her spoon through chunks of chicken, vegetables, and dumplings. The woman forced herself to take a bite.

"The dumplings are very good, Mother Quarry," she murmured in a monotone as she gazed into her bowl. "Of course, your cooking is always good."

Encouraged, Zadok perked up. "Mama does everything good, huh, honey?"

Tassy made no response, and she sensed her husband's disappointment.

Then, Mother Quarry broke the glum silence, as she addressed her son, "So when are you going back?"

"I'll be leaving in the morning."

The old woman looked to Tassy. "He's going to go after those boys."

With a jerk, the wife lifted her head and gawked at her husband. "What for?"

Tassy's heart began to race as Zadok, once again, explained his reasons: vindication, dignity, justice.

Gideon interrupted his father. "Can I go, with you?"

"No, son."

"Why not, Pop? You'll need help! There are three of them!"

Scowling, Mother Quarry chided her grandson, "You were worked over once, boy! Isn't that enough?"

"No!" Gideon defiantly frowned. "I'm not afraid!" Then, his face lit up as he grinned. "I do pretty good with a chunk of firewood!"

His father smiled with amusement and pride at the boy. "I know you do, son. But this is something I have to do myself."

With her fingertips against her temples, Tassy shook her bowed head. "It won't do any good; it won't do..." She hid her face, in her hands. It was futile to try to eradicate the effects of the violation. Revenge would not make the misery go away. In fact, the situation would be made worse if her husband were arrested, maimed, or killed.

Mother Quarry went to Tassy, stood behind her, and wrapped her arms about her daughter-in-law's shoulders. Then Zadok knelt beside his wife. He caressed her lower back with one hand, while the other rested on her forearm.

"Mama," Zadok looked up, to the old woman, "would you brew Tassy a cup of tea?" Nodding, his mother went to the stove.

Zadok urged his wife to her feet and led her into the living room, directing her to the sofa. As she sat, her husband settled next to her. He wrapped an arm around her slouched shoulders and held her hand. Then, he kissed her cheek. But when he pulled her to him, Tassy pushed away.

"Zadok, you mustn't do this!" Her brow creased. "You'll just get hurt, if not killed! And that will only make matters worse!"

"Tassy," Zadok appealed to her, "I've explained why I have to do this! I'm sorry, honey, but I have to!" Her husband cupped her hands in his. "But I will be back, I promise. And then—then, we can go away. We can go to California, where your folks now live. I can always find work. I can build another house, a better one." Zadok stroked her raven black hair and assured her, "When I finish in town, I can load up our belongings in the truck, and come straight back here. You probably wouldn't want to go back to our house, anyway."

Anxiously, the man looked into his wife's anguished face, awaiting a response. She just stared at the floor.

Then, she began chanting. "No, no, no, no..."

Mother Quarry entered the room with a cup of tea for her daughter-in-law, and a cup of coffee for her son. With two steaming cups in his hands, Gideon followed. After the old woman handed her children their beverages, she took the proffered cup from Gideon. Then, with a scowl, she peered into the cup remaining in the boy's grasp.

Turning, she challenged her son, "You let the boy drink coffee?"

Zadok sheepishly raised his eyebrows and attempted to appease his mother. "Just a little, every once in a while."

Mother Quarry grumbled, "Well, I don't know."

She settled in her armchair. Gideon asked if they could watch television. His grandmother consented. "The Adventures of Ozzie and Harriet" was airing. With folded arms, Tassy sat, brooding, while observing the inane predicament that faced the

Nelson family. If only every family's problems could be so simple and harmless; if only they could be so simply resolved.

But the television programming did serve to occasionally distract the woman from her own woes, until the station signed off the air for the night. As Gideon turned off the set, she watched the displayed test pattern vanish into a minute white dot that faded to nothing.

Zadok took his wife by the hand and led her to the bedroom upstairs. There, in the dark, Tassy undressed. Automatically, she slipped out of her dress and undergarments and stood nude, facing the curtained window. Then, she realized what she had done.

The woman had always slept nude, under the bed covers, with her husband, delighting in the feel of his warm, smooth hard body against her sensual flesh. But this night was different. Tassy wanted to conceal herself in her garments and hide under the covers. She wasn't deserving of her husband's touch or affection. However, after a pause of indecision, she elected not to bother re-dressing. Instead, she crawled under the covers, facing the window and stared into the dark.

Tassy heard and felt her husband climb into the bed from the other side. Then, she felt the warmth of his body as he nestled his chest against her back and placed his arm across her body. His right hand rested on her left shoulder.

Tears welled in Tassy's eyes. Rather than rejecting her, the woman's husband still seemed to accept her. Perhaps he was just being charitable. But his welcoming embrace, his reassuring warmth, was yet a comfort to Tassy. And she basked in his embrace, until she drifted off to sleep.

Catching up, on much needed sleep, Zadok awoke late in the morning. He lay with his back to his wife. Tassy was still. The man turned over. His wife's shoulder and upper back were un-covered, smooth golden flesh against the white sheet. He kissed her neck and back. He kissed her shoulder. Then he slid over, pressing his body against her own, and kissed her cheek. Tassy didn't respond. She didn't move.

The man wanted to envelope his wife and make love to her. But he didn't dare proceed any further. Perhaps she was too sore and tender. Perhaps she was now adverse to sex. Whatever the case, he knew it was too soon. Zadok turned away. But as he did so, Tassy rolled onto her back and grabbed her husband's arm.

"Come here," she bade him.

The man turned, and bracing himself on his forearms, gently lay atop his wife's soft body. With a content grin, he peered into her lovely face as she cupped his jaw in her hands.

In earnest, Tassy asked, "What can I do to make you change your mind about leaving."

Sighing, Zadok dropped his head and rested it between her breasts.

He wanted to say, "Let's make love, and I will forget the whole thing." And he would let it go, while losing himself in the love and passion. But he knew he couldn't indefinitely dismiss his need for vindication.

The man groaned, "Nothing."

Tassy again cupped his face and lifted his head. She stared in-tensely into his eyes. "I don't want to lose you."

Zadok grinned. "You won't."

He gave her a gentle kiss on her mouth. Tassy wrapped her arms around his neck and pulled him to her. They held one another for an extended time. Zadok wanted to cover her body with kisses.

He wanted to ravish her. But he knew that this was not the time. So he rose and sat on the edge of the bed. Sliding over to him, Tassy knelt behind him and wrapped her arms over his shoulders and across his chest. As she held him, Zadok caressed his wife's arms.

Then, he gently removed her arms from about him and stood. It was time to get started. Zadok slipped into his clothes. While he finished dressing, Tassy climbed from the bed and stood behind him. Her husband turned and, facing her, appraised her nude figure. Taking her into his arms, he caressed the small of her back, then clutched her to him. Their eyes locked. And Zadok passionately pressed her lips with his own.

"I'm going to get this over with," he proclaimed, "then I'm coming back to you."

The man gave his wife a final kiss and a hug. Then he left the room. Descending the stairs to the kitchen, he found his mother at the counter. She glanced back to her son, then turned her back to him. "You're up, I see," she groused. "Now, I can make breakfast."

He wasn't getting used to the negative attitude his mother was directing towards him, but Zadok understood her cold behavior, just as he understood Tassy's desperation.

"I'm not going to eat, Mama. I'm just going to head on out."

He poured himself a cup of coffee and gulped the hot beverage down. Gideon entered the kitchen. At least he seemed chipper, Zadok thought to himself.

"Please, Pop," the boy pleaded one last time, "let me go with you!"

"No," the man answered, between gulps, "I need you to take care of your mother."

"Grandma can take care of her!"

Placing his hand on the boy's shoulder, Zadok explained, "Look, I plan on coming back. But should something happen and I can't, you will need to be the man who takes care of your mother."

Gideon hung his head. "Papa, you're going to need help."

"Your mother needs you more. And I need you here."

As the man drained the cup, Tassy, donned in her blue and white dress, solemnly descended into the kitchen. Zadok gazed upon her. She was beautiful. She was his delight.

He set the cup down. "I've got to go!"

The father, son, and husband hugged his boy, then his mother, who shrugged him off, and then went to his wife. Zadok embraced and kissed her. His family followed him to the front door. At the threshold, Tassy grabbed her husband's face in her hands. Her gaze was penetrating and earnest.

"You take care, Zadok Quarry." She threw her arms around his neck and clung to him. "I want you back!"

The man grinned with delight, contrasting his wife's solemnity.

Zadok's spirits soared as he drove back towards town. He reveled in the brightness of the day, in the warmth of the sunshine, in the blueness of the sky, in the cornucopia of scents and aromas; poplar and pine, blackberries and marigolds, okra, corn and sorghum, and in the cacophony of birdsong: blue jays, black birds, finches and sparrows. He told himself that things were going to be alright. His wife still loved him and wanted him back. Her love was his strength and vitality.

But then, the man sobered when he contemplated his tactics in finding and confronting the villains who damaged his family. There was a great risk in what Zadok intended to do. His insides began to flutter with anxiety. His heart began to race as the truck neared the edge of town. Tightly gripping the steering wheel, the man's palms began to sweat.

Passing between Darky Town and the lumberyard, the driver sucked in a deep breath and blew it out. Zadok nervously tapped the steering wheel with the tips of his fingers. He passed the cafe and the motel, the gas station and the soda shop, the bank and the repair shop.

The man pulled up next to the bakery, and sat there, summoning up his nerve. Then, climbing out of the cab, Zadok walked over and stood in front the big window next to the bakery. He peered through the glass pane between the gold letters edged in red that read, "Royal's Barber Shop".

The black man spied Osmond Royal standing behind the barber chair, clipping the hair of a draped customer. Two other men sat in chairs along the wall.

Zadok turned from the window and stood, contemplating. Osmond Royal was not only the town barber, but he was also the Exalted Cyclops of the local clavern. More than likely, Zadok would run into opposition, maybe even into an altercation, should he confront the man. Hesitantly, the man questioned his intentions. Perhaps, Tassy was right; pursuing this course of action could prove to be futile—and fatal. He may even bring more hardship on his family. His retaliation against the rapists may result in retaliation against his wife and son. His was a doomed cause, anyway. He was a black man, after all. It would be best to turn around and drive back to his mother's house. His family would be pleased. They all opposed his intentions, anyway. He was alone in his determination to vindicate his family.

The man made the slightest move to walk away. But then, he caught himself and shook his head, as if to dispel such a consideration. He was being a coward, letting his fear get the best of him, hiding behind excuses. Zadok had to take a stand. He had to battle the suppression and degradation that was forced upon him and his own. Better to fight and die with his fists doubled and his chin up than to just take it, with his face in the dirt. His father died with his pride and dignity intact. Zadok would do the same for his son.

Besides, his family was in a safe place. And, if need be, they could flee to California, where Tassy's parents lived, a progressive state, that seemed more accepting and tolerant than most.

With a deep resolute breath, Zadok threw back his broad shoulders, clenched his jaw and, strode to the door of the barber shop. A bell tinkled as the black man pushed open the door. Four pairs of scrutinizing eyes gawked at him.

Scowling, Osmond Royal growled, "I don't cut no nigger-hair!"

As the barber dismissed him, Zadok persisted, explaining, "I'm not here for a hair cut, Mr. Royal. I just want to ask you a question or two."

Jabbing his scissors in the black man's direction, Osmond added, "I don't have niggers in my place, neither!"

With a crooked grin, the barber looked over to his seated customers. "Even my cleaning boy is white!"

The waiting men snickered, as did the plump man seated, draped in a striped apron, in the barber's chair.

Feeling somewhat agitated, Zadok crossed the shop and stood next to Osmond, who, in turn, glared balefully at him.

"Look, Mr. Royal," the black man's brow furrowed, his voice deepened, "my wife was raped night before last by three...by three white boys. My son was beaten..."

Osmond nearly jabbed Zadok in the face, as he once more gestured with his scissors and snapped, "I don't care about your high-yeller bitch or your pickaninny..."

Before the barber could say another word, Zadok had snatched up a straight razor and, sidling over behind him, pressed the gleaming blade against Osmond's throat. Instantly, the barber's rage turned to fear. His eyes bulged as Osmond craned his chin up into the air.

After the initial shock wore off, the customer seated nearest to the door leapt up and dashed out of the shop. His neighbor also sprang to his feet, but remained and gawked where he stood. When the customer in the barber's chair cranked his head about, he saw the razor at Osmond's throat, a ribbon of scarlet trickling down the barber's pale neck. The plump man sprang from his seat and gaped from a safe distance.

Through bared teeth, Zadok hissed, "Looky here, you nigger-hating, chalky-faced, lily white-assed son of a bitch, I care about my high-yeller wife and my pickaninny son! And what I want to know is, if the klan had anything to do with the attack on them!"

"No! No!" Osmond whined, his bugged eyes straining, as he stared down at Zadok's razor-wielding hand.

The customer near the wall barked, "You're a dead nigger, boy!"

"Shut up, Hilby!" demanded the man, draped in the striped apron, his eyes fixed on the black man and his victim.

Zadok snarled, "You know who the boys were, the ones who attacked my family?"

"No! No!" Osmond insisted. "I don't know anything about it!"

The assailant applied more pressure to the razor and persisted, "You sure?"

"Yes! Yes!" The barber accentuated his insistent reply with convulsive abbreviated nods of his head.

The black man had concluded his first inquiry. He had committed himself; he had stepped to the edge of the abyss. And there was no turning back. He had sealed his fate, whatever that would be. The question was, would he have the time to find the culprits and confront them before he was stopped.

He contemplated cutting his captive's throat.

The tall, slim deputy sat with his boots propped up on the desk, and the phone receiver to his ear. His pale blue eyes sparkled beneath his brunette brows. And a white smile crossed his handsome face, dimpling his cheeks.

"It's been over a week, Debbie Jo! I figured we could go see a

movie and then go back to my place, for a dip in the honey pot!"
He chuckled. "...I'm not being vulgar, sweetheart, I'm being cryp-
tic...No, dear. Vulgar would be suggesting that we go back to my
place to fuck...Oh lord, don't be so prudish!" His grin widened.
"You're not so prim and proper, in the sack!"

The man sat up, dropping his feet to the floor, his elbow resting on the desk. "Well, tell your mama that you'll be with the
law...Wait a minute! My reputation...It's over-exaggerated...Now,
don't go listening to Maggie Jean, or any of those other gals;
they're just envious..."

He raised his thick brows. "Well, are you sure?... Aw...well,
okay then. Some other time. Goodbye, sweetheart."

He disconnected and started to dial another number. "Hell,
I'll try Maggie Jean."

Just then, a man dashed through the door.

"J.J.," he gasped, "there's a crazy buck-nigger at Ozzie's! He's
holdin' a knife on 'im!"

The deputy sat up. "Ozzie's got a razor on him?"

"No! No!" The informant grimaced. "The buck's got the
razor on Ozzie!"

Rising to his feet, J. J. grumbled, "Ah, good lord."

With long strides, the lawman passed through the office door
and headed for the cruiser parked at the curb. Using his hand as a
fulcrum, he hurdled over the hood. J.J. slid into the driver's seat
and started the engine. Then he sped to the corner and skidded
onto Main Street. The deputy whipped his car around the blue
GMC and jerked to a halt in front of the barber's shop. Marching
into the shop, his thumbs tucked in his black leather holster, the
deputy quickly surveyed the scene.

"Hilby, Chet, get out!"

Ripping the apron from around him, Chet obeyed and followed Hilby out of the door. J.J. heard and spied, from the corner
of his eye, a crowd beginning to form in front of the window and

before the door. He stepped into the center of the shop and leveled his cool blue eyes on the big black man, whose eyes and weapon remained on the captive, like a wolf worrying a trembling hare. The deputy furrowed his brow. He recognized the black man, whom he had occasionally seen around town. J.J. had been impressed by the man's appearance and bearing.

"Isn't your name Zadok Quarry?" the lawman asked.

The smoldering dark eyes glanced over to J.J., then returned to Osmond's throat. As if futilely reaching for the razor, the lawman raised his left hand, while lowering his right nearer his pistol.

"Now, boy, I want you to lower that blade. You haven't done any real harm yet," he said, with little conviction, noticing the thin lines of blood striping the barber's neck. "So just put the razor down."

The glowering eyes glanced once more to J.J., then back to the captive. With a sneer, Zadok took the streaked blade away from Osmond's bleeding neck. Then he shoved the barber away from him. Osmond stumbled on his feet, while the black man dropped the razor. The blade clanged on the tiled floor.

"Good," the deputy purred, letting out a relieved breath. "Now come on over here, so's we can talk."

His eyes narrowing, Zadok started across the room and headed for the door. As he was about to pass J.J., the lawman stepped forward, reached out, and grabbed the man's forearm. With clenched teeth, Zadok yanked his arm from the deputy's grasp and shoved him. Stumbling back into the chairs along the wall, J.J. fell on his butt. He rose to one knee. With an irritated growl, he pulled his pistol from the leather holster, aiming at the brooding black man.

"Damn it, boy!" J.J. rasped. "Hold it right there, or I'll shoot!"

Glaring at the lawman, as if measuring him up, Zadok finally relaxed his broad shoulders, and allowed an impish grin to soften his stern countenance. The deputy rose to his feet, keeping a wary eye, and the gun barrel, fixed on the man.

"Turn around, boy, and put your hands behind you."

Zadok complied. He was cuffed and led out of the door, to face a mob of curious and reproving white folk. They were like a flock of carrion birds, eager to fall upon a carcass. J.J. ordered the onlookers to make room. Clearing a narrow path, they formed a gauntlet from the shop door to the cruiser. The crowd murmured; some shouted and cursed. A young woman leaned towards the two, her brown ponytail bobbing behind her, and spat on the black man. Grimacing, J.J. put his hand on her shoulder and gently pushed her back. "Jesus, Bessie!" he reproached her.

The young woman was one of the deputy's fresh-faced "love interests". But her ignorant display disgusted him.

"That nigger's a dead man!" someone from the crowd shouted.

"Wait 'til ol' Ozzie gets a hold on him!" another added.

Opening the back door of the car, the lawman urged his prisoner inside the cruiser and closed the door. Then he gazed over the loathing faces.

"Like a bunch of damned animals," he grumbled to himself, stepping around to the driver's side of the car.

Climbing, into his seat, J.J. turned over the engine and pulled away from the curb, leaving the angry mob behind.

As he drove, the lawman asked, "Man, what got into you? Don't you know that Ozzie Royal is a Cyclops, in the Klan?"

"Yes," the prisoner muttered, staring out of the side window. "That's why I wanted to talk to him."

"What?" J.J. frowned in puzzlement. "What the hell for? Are you crazy?"

In a low monotone, Zadok continued, "My wife was raped, and my son was beaten."

The deputy fell silent for a moment. Then he swore under his breath. He hated brutality, regardless against whom it was committed.

J.J. asked, "And you think Ozzie did it?" He smirked. "He wouldn't lay his hands on a Negro—not directly." Shifting in his seat, the lawman threw his arm over the back of the passenger's seat, and looked back. "But you think Ozzie had something to do with it?"

"Possibly."

J.J. shook his head then turned the corner. "Well, that was no way to try to find out; they'll kill you for that!" He snorted. "My god, you cut the man's throat! I mean, you didn't kill 'im, or even hurt 'im much, but you drew blood!"

Once again, the lawman shook his head, then smirked. "Man, a Negro laying hands on Ozzie Royal—cutting his throat, yet!" J. J. mused in silence. Then he told his charge, "I'll have to transfer you somewhere—but where? I don't know." The deputy sighed. "They'll probably storm the jail and lynch you! And, if Sheriff Platt was in town, he'd let 'em do it!"

J.J. pulled the cruiser up to the curb in front of the sheriff's office. A couple of men, standing on the sidewalk, stared, while the lawman led his prisoner inside. Passing the desk, J.J. uncuffed his charge and, as the prisoner stepped into the cell, closed the door with a clang.

Walking over to a small table set against the wall, the deputy picked up a cup from the red gingham table cloth and the coffee pot from the hot plate. He poured himself a cup.

He turned to his prisoner. "Care for some coffee?"

"Please."

"Take anything in it?"

"No, sir. I drink it black."

As he poured another cup and brought it to the black man, J.J. inquired, "You are Zadok Quarry, right?"

"Yes, sir."

"Just call me J.J.; everybody else does." He pulled a chair from around the desk and faced it towards the cell. The lawman sat and propped up his feet on the cell door cross bar. "Call me 'sir', and I won't know who you're talking to." J.J. grinned then sipped his beverage.

Standing at the bars with his cup in his hand, the black man replied, "Alright. But I never called a white man by anything other than his last name proceded with 'sir', much less by his initials."

"Yeah, I know." The deputy dropped his feet and sat up. "I hear you're a good man, Zadok—hardworking, good character. Some say you're too prideful, for a Negro, but as ol' Abe said, 'You can't please all of the people all of the time.'"

Each man took a swallow of coffee.

Then, J. J. continued, "Your daddy was killed years ago, wasn't he?"

"Yes."

"Shot right off of his mule one evening! A money dispute, wasn't it?"

"I reckon."

The lawman sighed. "Well, I think you're gonna end up like your daddy. It's bad enough that you attacked a white man, but Ozzie Royal..."

"Royal's a coward." Zadok scowled.

Looking up from his cup, J. J. remarked, "Yeah, but when he's hiding under his sheet, and has his mob behind him; he struts and crows plenty!"

During the interlude, the deputy assessed his charge. J.J. was indifferent to the colored; he had nothing against them, but he hardly had anything to do with them either. Like many folk, the lawman considered the Negro as a lower class, not quite a sub-human species, somewhere between apes and men, but inferior. He saw no harm in letting Negroes drink from the same fountains as did whites, or in using the same toilets.

After all, even should a black woman enter through the back door of a white family's home, she was entering the same space. She would have access to most of the house, if not all of it. She would clean the house, cook the meals, often bathe the white children. In the old days, black women were even put to nursing white infants! The "Jim Crow" regulations weren't about sanitary concerns, they was about suppressing the Negro, about keeping him in his place. And he hated to hear about cases of needless abuse committed against Negroes. They had feelings the same as did whites, though they may be somehow inferior.

However, as he faced the black man in the cell, J.J. saw a man of intelligence and sensibility, in spite of the actions that had placed him behind bars. He was a man that projected confidence and determination. He stood erect, with his shoulders back and his eyes forward. And he was apparently a man with passion. Zadok obviously had a deep affection for his family. He seemed to be an exceptional specimen of his race.

Studying the brooding man, the lawman inquired, "Did your wife recognize her attacker?"

Smoldering eyes met his gaze. "There were three. But no, my wife didn't recognize them. I don't think they were from around here. That's why I thought the Klan might have been behind the attack."

J.J. hunched forward. "Well, if Ozzie knows anything about it, he won't tell you." Rubbing his square chin, the deputy stood. "Did your wife remember anything that might help identify the men; did she hear any names, see any distinctive marks, anything about what they wore or what they drove?"

"They stunk of liquor. Maybe they obtained bootleg from around here; maybe that's what they were doing in this vicinity."

"Yeah, that sounds logical," J.J. agreed. He looked to the prisoner. "I know a few local moonshiners."

Zadok continued, "They were young men. The leader was a big fellow. My son remembered that he work a black and tan jacket with an emblem of a red razorback on the back."

The deputy perked up. "Almaville!"

"What?"

"Almaville! The razorback is the school mascot! They must have been..."

Hearing the door squeak on its hinges, J. J. turned to find Osmond Royal walking in, with a big smile on his face and a bandage under his jaw. The lawman felt a twinge of dread.

"Hey J.J.," the barber's tone was chipper, "you can let that man out of that cell. I'm not going to press charges."

His fists on his hips, the lawman replied, "You're not?"

Osmond wagged his head. "No. The man was overwrought; his family had been attacked! I sympathize with him."

J.J. arched a brow. "You, sympathize with a Negro?"

The barber's smile lost some of its flourish. "I'm not pressing charges, J.J.; you can let him go."

Taking a deep breath, the lawman stated, "Well, I think I'll just keep him locked up for the night—let him cool off."

A hardness came over Osmond's eyes. His smile strained.

His voice was low and adamant. "He's cool. Let him go."

Then his face seemed to brighten and his smile widened, as the barber approached the cell and addressed the prisoner. "No hard feelings, huh?"

Zadok sternly peered back at the man. "Do you know who attacked my family?"

"Why, I'm afraid I don't." Osmond seemed apologetic. "But if I did, I'd be glad to help you out!"

He turned his exaggerated smile to J.J. "I oppose senseless violence towards our darkies. Uppity niggers need to be controlled and need to be put in their place. But good niggers, like this fella—I hate to see them suffer unnecessarily."

The lawman narrowed his eyes and pinched his lips. "Yeah, I'm sure you do!"

His sarcasm seemed lost on Osmond, as the barber crossed the office.

Pausing at the door, Osmond turned. "Let him go home and comfort his family."

The door closed.

Alarmed, J.J. jerked about and faced his charge. "Where is your family?"

The brooding man answered, "They are safe. I took them out of town, to my mother's house."

Releasing a deep sigh, the deputy relaxed his frame. "I'm gonna hold you overnight. In the morning, I can escort you—"

"You said they might storm the jail and take me anyway."

"They might. But they might also know that they'd have a fight on their hands. I'd kill to protect my prisoners and my office. And Sheriff Platt isn't here to keep me in check."

"No," Zadok countered. "Let me out. I'll have to face him and his bunch sooner or later. I can't leave town until I find out who hurt my family."

"Zadok, you're colored!" J.J. argued. "What good would it do to pursue this? Nothing will be done about it, if you do find those boys!"

The black man's eyes smoldered. "I intend to do something about it!"

The lawman shook his bowed head.

"Just let me out," Zadok insisted. "I have to get to the drugstore before it closes."

J.J. raised his head and wrinkled his nose. "The drugstore! What for?"

"I need to get some balloons."

The deputy gaped. "Balloons?"

Zadok clarified, "Balloons."

Osmond sat against the door in the cab of the lead truck. Another loaded pick up followed. He had been informed that Zadok Quarry had been released and had returned to his home. So, the Cyclops, and over a dozen of his Klan associates, headed for the secluded house.

At the foot of the dirt road leading to the black man's place, the trucks stopped, and the men, in the beds of the trucks, slipped on their white hoods, and the riders in the cabs stepped out, donning their hoods and robes. The barber insisted on the wearing of full regalia, as this was a significant occasion. That buck-nigger's transgression was extreme; to humiliate and degrade Osmond, an Exalted Cyclops, in that way, to lay hands on him and threaten him, to draw blood in his own shop, with his own razor... The nigger's arrogance overwhelmed Osmond. And the nigger would pay.

He imagined the torture that they would put the black man through. First, they would scare the bejesus out of him. They would make the coon piss his britches and sweat like a roasting pig. All bug-eyed, he'd cry and beg for mercy. And Osmond would show none. Let the arrogant uppity nigger suffer. The Cyclops would have Zadok stripped. And while the coon stood naked and trembling, Osmond would have him beaten, until he dropped to his knees, then have him kicked and stomped.

Then he'd have the nigger's pickaninny brought before him, so he could watch his son being beaten, kicked, and stomped. Then his high-yeller bitch would be brought forth. She would be repeatedly raped and beaten, before her nigger husband's eyes. Hell, that buck thought his family had been abused before... Osmond would have the uppity bastard flayed, have the boys piss on him. They would tar and feather him. Then they would lynch the black bastard and set him afire.

The Cyclops licked his lips, as if savoring the taste of vengeance.

The humble house came into sight. Zadok's pick-up was parked near the corner of the porch, opposite the side where the garage set. The stupid nigger didn't run. Osmond leered with malicious satisfaction. Maybe the buck figured it would be best just to get it over with. But he was going to wish that he had run; he'd wish he had run as far away as he possibly could.

The trucks pulled up to the front of the house, skidding to a halt along the shoulder of the oval driveway. The house was dark; no lights on inside or out. And, while the gang climbed out of the trucks and assembled in a line before the house, Osmond could imagine the family cowering in the darkness. Torches were handed out, and the Cyclops took one. The fuel tipped staves were lit with a taper as the holder walked along the line of eager klansmen. The darkness receded with the igniting of each flaring torch. The flames danced in the slight breeze like agitated spirits. Fire symbolized purging and purity. It also symbolized avenging and resolute wrath. Osmond stepped forward, his chest puffed up with superiority and power.

He held his burning torch in his right hand, as he cupped his left hand around his mouth and bellowed. "Nigger Quarry! Come on out here, you buck-nigger! Retribution is at hand and about to rain on your woolly black head!" The Cyclops' body quivered with excited anticipation. "Come on, boy! Save your family! We just want you! Don't be a black-assed coward!"

The house remained dark and silent.

Another klansman shouted, "Come on, nigger, 'fore we put your cracker box to the torch!"

The gang silently waited. Only the crackling flames broke the quiet. The Cyclops began to wonder if Zadok had run. He felt disappointment. Perhaps his vengeance would be delayed.

He was about to give orders to have the house and the property searched when, from his peripheral vision, Osmond spied a sphere rocketing towards him from his left. In a split second, he noticed a sheen on the edge of the descending smooth orb. Clutching his torch, the Cyclops defensively crossed his arms in front of his face, as he anticipated a solid and painful impact. But, to Osmond's surprise, he barely felt the force, as the missile smashed into him with a splat. He was also surprised when the orb seemed to explode, and he found himself engulfed in roaring flames. Shrieking, and dropping his torch, the inundated klansman flailed and stomped his feet in a comical dance. He felt the excruciating pain of his left arm burning. Osmond screamed in agony, as the unbearable sensation traveled over his shoulder, down his side, and across his chest. His hood caught fire. In a panic, the Cyclops tore the hood from his head, sparing his face worse than second degree burns. But his torso still burned. His robe blackened and began to disintegrate into flakes of ash.

Recovering from the shock, other klansmen gathered about the human torch and began swatting at the flames. Osmond felt faint and disoriented; he felt as though he were in a dream world. This was a horrible nightmare, not reality. The Cyclops was knocked off of his feet. He felt as though he was whirling on a speeding carousel, while he was being rolled back and forth on the ground. Osmond was unaware of the handfuls of dirt being thrown over him.

His robe was finally extinguished, and the commotion died down. He lay, dazed, in the remnant of his scorched and blackened robe, in his charred shirt and trousers coated with dirt. His blistered and blackened arms were caked with dust. The victim felt as though his flesh had been peeled away, exposing his screaming nerves. Severe pain radiated through his upper body and face. The Exalted Cyclops cried out, when his robe and shirt were peeled away, sticking to and pulling at his seared flesh. He was barely aware of the moans of awe, and the curses, expressed by his cohorts, as his bare skin was exposed.

Dispirited, his associates pulled off their hoods from their hanging heads. Some slithered out of their robes. Osmond began a new chorus of anguished cries, when he was lifted and carried to one of the truck beds, where a blanket had been laid out. Under the pressure of grasping hands, the victim's body again felt as though on fire. He was placed on the blanket. About him, sat the disheartened men. The Cyclops felt the jostling of the pick-up, while it made its way from Zadok's turnout to the road that led to the highway. With each bump and jolt, searing pain shot through the pitiful klansman's damaged body.

Zadok sat on the edge of the seat of the weathered picnic table beside his pickup. From there, he had watched as the loaded trucks had skittered along the drive and pulled out of the oval of dirt that served as his driveway. Peering over the hood of his pickup, the man had chuckled to himself.

"The Keystone Klansmen." He grinned.

He congratulated himself on his marksmanship. Earlier that evening, he had strategically parked his truck near the edge of the porch and moved the picnic table from under the elm tree to the side of his pickup. From his vantage point, the man had a clear view of his porch and most of the front yard and driveway. Yet, he was concealed. Zadok began with water balloons. Like a human catapult, he had flung the swollen orbs from the blade of his shovel at specific targets. When he was satisfied with his accuracy, the man then filled several balloons with gasoline, pushed through a spray pump.

It couldn't have gone better. As the trucks roared up to his yard, and the robed mob assembled, Zadok couldn't help but to tense up. His stomach fluttered. But his anxiety gave way to anger, while he had listened to the villain's threats and demands. They looked like a pack of arrogant ghosts. And they called colored people 'spooks'! he thought to himself. Zadok knew there would be fire; there always was fire.

With satisfaction, he recalled the episode; clutching the spade handle near the blade, with one hand, the man had placed a swollen balloon on the steel head, then placed his free hand farther down the handle. With a wide grip, he had felt he had good control of his weapon. His body tingled with renewed anxiety when he eyed his target, the Exalted Cyclops. Zadok had calculated the distance and location. Taking a nervous breath, the man had launched his missile and watched it arc through the darkness, towards the target, and watched the orb splat over the Cyclops, who was instantly engulfed in flames. Zadok had nearly leaped with elation, for the execution was perfect.

The commotion that followed was like watching a comical short at a movie house—Buster Keaton or Charlie Chaplain.

Savoring his victory, the man proceeded to drain the remaining balloons.

Zadok awoke in the mid-morning. Though his previous night had been victorious and gratifying, the man had been anxious and restless. And his sleep was fitful. With a gaping yawn, Zadok sat up on the sofa, where he had slept for the rest of the night, and stretched his corded arms above his head. As he sat, the man's eyes closed. His chin sank to his chest. And before long, Zadok was snoring.

Then, a knock at his door roused him. The man's wary eyes shifted to the sound. Suspiciously, he crept over to the front window and peered out, spying a patrol car parked in front of the yard. Either the deputy or Sheriff Platt was at his door. Zadok hoped it would be J.J. Opening the door, his relief was evident to the deputy, who stood before him with an impish grin on his handsome face.

"Mornin', Mr. Quarry!" J.J. cheerily greeted, pushing a wisp of dark hair back in place. "You don't look the worse for wear, considering all the commotion that went on up here last night!"

"I had no trouble," Zadok mumbled.

Raising his brows in mock wonder, the lawman exclaimed, "Well, the Klan sure did, especially ol' Ozzie Royal! That son of a bitch looks like a mulatto now, only the black is mostly on the left side of his body!" J.J. chuckled. "He lost his left eye and his left arm. The doctors are worried about infection setting in."

Stone-faced, the black man was silent, while his visitor seemed to be anticipating a reaction.

Finally, Zadok asked, "Are you here to arrest me?"

The deputy's eyes widened, again feigning wonder. "Arrest you—for what?" As if looking back at the fools in town, J.J. turned his head, and gazed behind him. "Everyone is in awe! Some of the kluxes say a fire ball dropped from the sky and fell right on Ozzie, bursting and engulfing him in flames! A few think he just spontaneously erupted into a blaze! Either way, nearly all think it was supernatural!"

Again, the lawman seemed to await a response. But his host gave nothing away. Then, J.J. continued, "Some folks say your guardian angel was looking out for you; others say you called upon the forces of darkness!"

"Not likely, in either case," Zadok muttered.

The two stood in silence.

Then, the lawman stated, "Well, I'm glad to see that you're okay." A grin crossed J.J.'s face. "Oh, did you get your balloons?" A glint showed in his eye as the deputy's grin widened.

Zadok suppressed a smile. "Yes."

"They come in handy?" J.J.'s face turned sober. "May I come in? I'd like to talk to you."

Stepping aside, the black man allowed his visitor to enter. As he led his guest to the kitchen, the host offered, "Would you like a piece, of strawberry-rhubarb pie?"

J.J. settled in a dining chair, his hands resting on his thighs. "Strawberry-rhubarb, huh? Sure."

Zadok went to the refrigerator.

"You have a nice place here," the guest observed. "It's simple but homey."

"It's high class for a colored family around these parts."

Laying the pan with half of a pie on the counter (he had eaten the other half the night before as a sort of celebration treat, his first meal since eating supper at his mother's house), he cut the remainder of the fare, equally, in two. He scooped the slices onto plates and set a piece before the deputy.

Taking a bite, J.J. remarked, "Yes, sir! That's tasty!"

"Mrs. Baird baked it," Zadok stated. "I was working for Mr. Baird the night my family was attacked."

"The Bairds are good people," the lawman claimed between chews.

"Yes, they are. Mr. Baird has always dealt fairly with me."

Swallowing, J.J. leaned on the table. "You are obviously an intelligent man, capable of handling yourself." He leaned back in his chair. "Maybe, last night, you were just lucky." He studied his host. "But I can see that you can handle yourself."

The guest took another bit of pie and talked around the bite. "You still want to pursue this thing?"

"Yes," Zadok assured him.

"Well, I know a couple of moonshiners I can talk to. That's a start, anyway."

He looked to the black man. "What do you plan on doing?"

"I plan on going into town, making inquiries."

"Would you wait 'til I get back into town; wait 'til tomorrow?"

Zadok shrugged.

J.J. went on, "You got the townsfolk spooked. They may not give you any trouble; they may try to stay clear of you. But think about the Salem witch hunts. Some may try to grab you and burn you at the stake!"

The lawman rubbed his finger along his chin. "I need to be discreet in helping you with your investigation. But, perhaps, I can watch your back some. I'll help you get there, so just be patient. Besides, I may find out all we need to know, before I get back into town, okay?"

The black man gave a nod. He would welcome the deputy's unexpected assistance. But he couldn't sit still and wait. Zadok had to act.

Like a wary stag, J.J. skulked through the pine and cedar timber. He stepped lightly over clutters of leaves, needles, and twigs on the wooded floor. In an attempt at stealth, the lawman was even wearing his tennis shoes on this occasion. He wanted to take the moonshiner by surprise, but he knew that the man he was seeking was sly and alert.

Peering through the wood, J.J. spotted the cabin. Breathing slow and shallow, the deputy prowled on. He spied youngsters playing about the homestead. Then J.J. sensed a presence nearby. He rose from his crouched stance and slowly turned. And he could barely discern the almond-skinned bald figure, in denim overalls, with one strap hanging loose over the bib, among the timber, his ancient deer rifle pointed at the deputy.

With a disappointed sigh, J.J. cursed. "Damn you, Doe Cobb!"

Lowering the rifle butt, the barefoot, lanky man stepped out into the open. His tanned arms were thin and long, but sinewy.

The lawman grumbled, "You must have a hell of a nose."

"Well, you jest come crashin' through here like a blind and

lame mule." Doe grinned.

J.J. winced at the barb. The two walked together towards the cabin. As they came to the clearing, the deputy gazed on four children playing near the lodging. The youngest was a toddler; the eldest was about the right age for elementary school.

"How many kids you got now?"

"Had an even dozen, but I think a panther or bear dragged a few of 'em off." Doe sighed. "Well, they ain't much good fer nothin', anyhow." He turned to his visitor. "They do seem to keep the varmints down, though."

They began to amble on.

J.J. asked, "Where's your squaw?"

"Oh, the lusty bitch run off with an ol' sod buster not long ago."

Then, as if on cue, a young woman, her raven black hair fashioned in long braids, stepped out onto the porch. Her bright yellow floral dress complimented her bronze skin.

"Oh, there she is," Doe remarked, as if mildly surprised.

The lawman chuckled. "Looks like she came back."

"Yeah." Doe turned to his guest. "You wan' 'er?"

J.J. frowned. "Want her?"

"Yeah!" The host emphasized his reply with a furrowed brow and a vigorous nod of his bald head. "I charge a fella a dollar, but since you're an upstanding lawman, I'll charge you two."

The guest shook his head. "You're disgusting, Doe."

"Well, you brought it up!"

"Me?"

"Yeah! You were askin' after her, then eyin' 'er, like a starvin' fox findin' his self, before a hen house!"

The deputy grinned. "Doe, you're impossible."

"So you don't wan' 'er?"

"No!"

"Why not? What's wrong with 'er?"

"I dunno. But there's got to be something wrong with her, if she stays with you!"

The host feigned offense. "Aw, now that was jest rude, Jasper Jerrod White! It's sons o' bitches like you what make hospitality a chore!"

"And it's sons o' bitches like you that make cordiality a chore."

"Touche, Jasper Jerrod, touche."

They climbed the steps to the porch, where two rung-backed chairs sat. Each took a seat. Then Doe reached for the jug sitting next to his chair. Gazing over his children, rollicking about their mother, the moonshiner took a swig. Then, he handed the jug to his guest.

"Doe, I'm a man of the law!"

The host gave a slight shrug. "I won't hold it agin' ya."

J.J. didn't care for liquor. He would keep good wine on hand, at home, to offer to his female company, in order to relax their inhibitions. But he didn't care much for the taste of wine either. But, so as to placate his gracious host, the lawman took a slug, then grimaced.

"Pussy," Doe ridiculed the man.

J.J. complained, "If I were to spill any of this in your lap, I bet it would eat through your overalls, right down to your pecker!"

Taking the jug from the deputy, the host replied, "I use this to eat the rust off my corroded metals."

"I hate to think what this shit is doing to your insides!"

"My stomach is cast iron." Doe grinned. "And it's rust-free."

Doe's wife returned, with a toddler in her arms.

While she ascended the steps, J.J. nodded. "Ma'am."

Smiling demurely, she glanced at the deputy, then lowered her eyes.

As the woman passed through the door, Doe growled, "Get back in that house, and get something done, damn it! Quit tryin' to seduce the company!"

He scowled at the lawman. "Jasper Jerrod here has a busy enough pecker as it is!"

J.J. scowled back. "My reputation as a Casanova is greatly exaggerated!"

"I think the only exaggeration is how well endowed and how talented you are."

With furrowed brow, the lawman cocked his head. "And just who have you been talking to? Because I don't recall ever fucking you!"

The host sniggered.

Gazing over the yard, the deputy inquired, "So do your customers come all the way out here to get their liquor?"

"Oh, hell no! I have a rendezvous closer to town."

"Where at?"

Doe shot his guest a sly grin. "I ain't tellin' you!"

"Oh Christ, Doe, you know I wouldn't come down on you! Sheriff Platt would have my hide if I did!"

"Oh hell, Platt don't buy from me! He's too good for the likes of me! He buys his shine from upstanding characters, such as Skip Meadows or Pete Overland—even though my brew is better."

J.J. shifted in his seat. "So did you have any customers from out of the area a couple o' nights ago?"

The moonshiner shook his head.

The lawman pressed, "Would you tell me if you did?"

Doe grinned at his guest. "Jasper Jerrod, you know I would! If it has to do with somethin' important enough to get you to come all the way out here an' see me, I would."

The deputy felt his face warm. He was moved by his friend's loyalty.

"How about any local fellas recently?"

Frowning, Doe pondered a moment. "Yep, the Stover boy. He met up with me three nights ago."

J.J. looked over to the moonshiner. "Anyone else?"

"No. I met most of my customers at least a week ago. The Stover boy met me at Whitley's and asked to buy a jug."

"Anyone with him?"

"Nope."

Rising to his feet and clapping his friend on his bare shoulder, the lawman said, "Thanks, Doe. That's all I needed to know."

The moonshiner remained in his chair and watched his children play.

"You got a nice lookin' bunch o' kids, Doe."

"Yeah," he moaned. "They're alright. But it's too bad the squaw don't throw mules."

"Don't know why not." J. J. grinned. "She's teamed with a jackass."

Doe glared with mock offense. "Now that's just rude! Jasper Jerrod White, your mama ever teach you manners! Git, 'fore I blow another hole in your ass!"

Chuckling, the lawman descended the steps. "Give your squaw my best."

"Hell no! But I give 'er my best, on a reg'ler basis."

As J.J. headed into the timber, the moonshiner hollered after him, "I ought 'a send the savage with you! The mean ol' bitch would serve you right!"

"Hell, Doe," the deputy yelled back, "she's a good gal! She doesn't even say so much as a word!"

"Not to you! She saves it all up for me! Meaner than hell, I swear—chasin' after me, with knives an' shit! Hell, I had to confiscate her tommyhawk the other day!"

J.J. paused at the edge of the clearing. "You probably deserved it!"

He heard Doe chuckle. "You're probably right!"

"Take care, Doe Cobb!"

"Yeah! You too, Jasper Jerrod!"

As Zadok pulled into town, his gas gauge needle pointed a hair above empty. So he turned into the gas station. There, he sat. No one came out to serve him. The driver could see the attendant seated in front of the big window, glowering at him. Finally, Zadok climbed out of the cab and walked around to the pump.

As he stood with nozzle in hand, the attendant rushed out and hollered at the black man. "Hey, boy, put that back!"

Zadok looked down on the slim employee. "I need gas."

His hand on his hip, the attendant stated, "We're out!"

The black man gazed over at the station's sun streaked window, suspecting the attendant's response was a lie.

Then, he reached for his gas cap. "Do you mind if I try?"

Starting forward, the employee checked his momentum. He stood in place and nervously bounced on his toes. "Yes, I do mind! Are you callin' me a liar, boy?"

As Zadok glared down at him, the hardness in the attendant's gray eyes disappeared; the disdain was replaced with uncertainty. The slim man pulled a rag from his hip pocket and nervously twiddled it in his animated hands.

Sighing, the black man banged the nozzle back into its cradle. Then he returned to his seat and pondered. He needed gas. Zadok could siphon the fuel from someone's tank but from whom?

The black man was stirred from his musing when a pounding against his passenger's window alerted him.

The attendant had regained his bravado and scowled through the window, vehemently gesturing for the driver to leave. Zadok wanted to grab the man by his collar and shake him. But instead, the black man remained still. Then he thought of Dr. Orley. He was nearby, perhaps near enough. Starting up the truck, Zadok screeched his tires and sped out of the station onto the main street. He gave a smug smile, catching the attendant in his side mirror, shaking his upraised fist, and bobbing up in the air, angrily shouting.

Driving along Blue Jay Rd., the pickup started to lurch. And before he reached the corner of Black Willow St., the man's truck died and coasted to a halt.

Taking the gas can from the bed of his pickup, Zadok chided himself. "Should've filled up when leaving Mama's house."

He walked the half mile to the physician's place. With can in hand, the man walked up to the door and knocked. The doctor's blue eyes widened as he greeted his visitor.

"Zadok, good to see you!" He clapped the black man's shoulder and urged him inside. "Come in, come in!"

As the two men entered the parlor and sat, Dr. Orley inquired, "How are Tassy and Giddy?"

With a somber sigh, Zadok slumped his shoulders. "Well, Giddy is still tender." A smile started. "But his spirits seem to be recovering just fine."

The physician chuckled. "He's a brave boy."

"He is."

Then, the black man's expression sobered. "Tassy seems to be coming out of her—whatever it is."

He recalled her embrace and her words, as he was departing that day: "You take care, Zadok Quarry! I want you back!" He felt his face soften at the memory.

"How's your mama?"

His mother's irregular consternation towards him, while he was at her house, came to mind, and the black man grinned. "She's fine."

He turned to the doctor. "She's spunky!"

"She's quite a woman."

Then, a corner of Dr. Orley's mouth curled up under his silver mustache. "I heard about what happened, up at your place last night."

Brows raised, Zadok suppressed a satisfied smile.

The physician shook his head. "I'm not surprised. Mixing fire and all them bed sheets—I reckon it was bound to happen, sooner of later."

"I reckon," the black man echoed.

Glancing at the gas can beside his guest, Dr. Orley asked, "You run out of gas?"

Zadok explained his predicament. The doctor led his visitor outside to the driveway, where he allowed Zadok to siphon gas from the tank of his station wagon.

"Take all you need. I'll drive up to Delbert's and fill 'er up after. No doubt that weaselly Melvin is lying about having no gas."

Then, Dr. Orley drove the man back to his pickup, and wished him well, before heading to the gas station.

Zadok drained the fuel into his gas tank. But when he tried to turn over the engine, the result was a simple click. Raising the hood, the man found that his distributor cap was missing. Wires were splayed over the engine like giant spider legs. Zadok slammed the hood closed. Glaring into the windshield, a smile slowly spread over his face, though there was nothing actually humorous about the situation. He shook his head.

The tension released from his body and mind, the man moved to the cab and shifted the truck into gear. He grasped the steering wheel, leaned into the frame of the door, and began pushing the heavy vehicle down the road. Zadok began gasping. His muscles strained as he poured on speed in order to make the corner onto Black Willow St. Trudging around the curve, the man continued down the straight road. His stout thighs began to ache and his calves burned, while he dug the balls of his feet into the rough and weathered asphalt. The man pressed on, like a lone ox leaning into its yoke, straining against a great burden.

Zadok was relieved when the physician's house came into sight and was all the more encouraged the closer he progressed. Summoning a reserve of strength and energy, the weary man picked up speed, then leaped into the driver's seat, as he turned into the driveway, and coasted up to the garage door. His aching muscles throbbed as he wiped sweat from his forehead. Taking deep breaths, he rested in the cab. Then he stepped out, and began stretching his arms and legs and twisting his body about.

He was clutching the edge of the side panel, arching his back, when he spied Dr. Orley's black Nomad approaching. Zadok stood up, while the station wagon pulled up behind him. The tall lanky doctor climbed out of the car.

Towering over the vehicle's roof, he knitted his thick brows. "Is everything alright, Zade?"

The black man explained his predicament.

Dr. Orley sighed in annoyance and shook his head. "Of course, you can leave your truck here. In fact, we can push it right into the garage, for safe keeping."

"Thank you, doc. You don't know how much I appreciate your help. You have been so good to my family and me."

Modestly, the physician dismissed the praise with a wave of his hand. Then he asked, "Is there somewhere I can take you? Do you need a ride home?"

"No." Zadok hung his weary head. "I don't want to impose on you anymore than I already have."

"Nonsense! I have no patients at the moment. I'll just leave a note on my door. I am at your service."

Placing his hands on his hips, the black man gazed into the distance. "Well, I could use a ride over to Clarence Stover's place."

"Clarence Stover?"

"Yes, I need to talk to his boy."

"Alright," Dr. Orley replied. "Let's get your truck in the garage, for safe keeping."

The black Chevy Nomad pulled up beside the front edge of the yard. From the car, Zadok could see Clarence Stover working beside the rustic house and in front of the shed. Zadok climbed out of the car.

"You want me to wait?" the doctor asked.

"No, doc. I don't want to take any more of your time."

"It's nearly a four mile walk back to town, Zade! I'll park over by that ol' elm. I'll wait for you there. He may just run you off his property, before you get a chance to address your business!"

The black man smiled. "Alright, doc. I appreciate that."

With a wave, the physician maneuvered a U-turn, and drove up to the elm tree, about thirty yards away, on the far side of the road. Zadok took a deep anxious breath before walking up to Clarence. The cooper's son was the only "Bernie" that he knew of. Mr. Stover stood at the end of the dirt driveway, among scattered staves and metal rings, a mallet in hand, and a cigarette dangling from his mouth. As Zadok approached, the cooper looked up and curiously squinted at the visitor.

The black man recalled how Clarence had hired him once before to load kegs and crates onto a flat bed. Mr. Stover was aloof, but decent. The cooper brushed wood debris from his brown overalls. His olive shirt sleeves were rolled above his swollen forearms. His hands were thick. Nearly as tall as his black visitor, the stout, dusky-haired man looked Zadok in the eye.

His cigarette bobbed between his lips, as Clarence gave greeting. "Zadok."

The black man attempted a cordial smile but didn't quite achieve it. "Mr. Stover. So you remember me."

"I do." Taking a puff from his smoke, the cooper replied, "It's been a few years, but I remember. You're a good worker."

"Thank you, Mr. Stover."

"I don't have any work for you now."

"That's not why I'm here, sir." Zadok knitted his brows in uncertainty as he pressed on. "I would like to speak to your boy, Bernie."

Taking a final puff from his cigarette, the cooper flicked the butt into the dirt. "What about?"

"My family was attacked by some boys, who were from out of town. I think your boy might know them."

Clarence tossed his mallet near a pile of staves. "My boy wouldn't have nothin' to do with nothin' like that."

Zadok spied Bernie peeking out from behind the shed door that stood ajar.

He persisted. "Yes, sir. But I think he knows who the boys were. They mentioned his name. I just want to know who the boys were."

The black man tried to interpret the stern glare in the cooper's gray eyes. Clarence turned his head towards the shed. "Bernie, come on out here!" His voice was deep and commanding.

The boy stepped out from behind the shed door and approached. The tall, lanky, dark-haired boy stood next to the cooper, just a couple of inches short of his father's height. His thumbs were hooked in his denim pockets. Like his father, the blue-eyed boy had a stern visage. Zadok discerned disdain in the blue eyes.

Clarence stated, "Zadok wants to ask you somethin'"

Glaring, Bernie replied, "I don't have to talk to no nigger."

The cooper gave his son a gruff nudge on the back of the shoulder that shoved the boy forward.

"His family was hurt by some boys you might know. If you do, tell 'im who they are."

Bernie hung his head.

Then, Zadok ventured, "I just want to know the names of the

boys who attacked my family the night before last. One of them mentioned your name."

Surprised, the boy looked up, gaping.

Then, once again, lowering his head, he mumbled, "Monty Dinmont, Reggie Brisby, and Arvis Shelly." Bernie looked down at his feet, scuffing the dirt with his left shoe. "I met them at the school house." Pausing, he shrugged a shoulder. "They-they was talkin' 'bout how ugly niggers were." He sheepishly glanced at Zadok, then dropped his gaze. "Reggie said somethin' 'bout nigger babies bein' cute, 'til they growed up. And Monty said somethin' 'bout how ugly colored women were. But Reggie said a lot o' high-yeller niggers were perty."

Bernie licked his lips. With shoulders hunched, he again looked at the ground and mumbled, " I told 'em, 'bout-'bout your wife, 'bout how perty she was. Monty told me I was full o' shit. But I told 'em it was true. Monty said he wanted to see for himself and asked where 'bouts she lived. And I..."

The boy looked to Zadok with pleading in his eyes. "I didn't think— I had no idea— I didn't know they would go up there! I didn't know they would hurt her!"

The black man stood in brooding silence. His heart raced. He felt his face warm. He clenched his teeth behind his tight lips.

Zadok asked the repentant boy in an even tone, "Do you know where I can find them?"

Again, Bernie looked up with woeful eyes. "They live over in Almaville. I don't know 'zactly where. But they talk about a place called Stucky's. It's a pool hall. Seems they hang out around there a lot."

The visitor gave a grateful but somber nod. Then he turned and began plodding up the drive.

"Zadok!" Clarence called out after him.

The black man turned.

"I'm sorry," the cooper said.

Zadok responded with a second grateful but somber nod.

J.J. was stepping out of the cafe when he spotted Zadok walking towards him on the other side of the street.

The deputy jogged across the road and addressed the black man, "I thought I told you to wait at home!"

Zadok glared at the lawman.

"Alright, alright." With a wave of his hand, J.J. dismissed the issue.

Then he informed his companion, "Listen, I talked to a moonshiner I know. He didn't do business with any out-o'-towners, but he said the Stover boy bought whiskey from him, three nights ago. Now, it's possible that the kid knows the boys!"

"He does," Zadok muttered. "I just came from Stover's place."

Puzzled, the deputy frowned. "How did you know to go to Stover's?"

"Tassy had said that one of the boys mentioned the name 'Bernie'. The Stover boy is the only 'Bernie' that I know of."

J.J. pursed his lips into a frown. The wind had been taken out of his sails. But he shrugged it off.

Without a thought, the lawman grasped his companion by the back of his arm and walked along with him. "Did you get their names?"

"Yes."

J.J. halted in his tracks. "Now what are you gonna do?"

"I'm going to Almaville to face them."

"And then what?"

Zadok looked away. "I don't know," he grumbled. He knew that he wanted to kill them, to tear them apart.

Pushing against the black man's shoulder, the lawman urged Zadok to turn and face him. "Okay, this is a pivotal moment here; you've got the information you were after. You know where to find the boys. Now, you have to decide whether or not you want to see this through. Once you find these boys, once you confront them, there will be no turning back."

J.J. licked his lips. "Look, I have an idea how you must feel, but you've got to think—is this something worth dying for? Regardless of what you do, those boys, or somebody else, might end up killing you! They will probably at least bust you up pretty bad, maim, or cripple you!"

He pinched his lips together. "I mean, so far, you've gotten away with what you did to Ozzie! Of course, no one knows what really happened that night but you." Arching a brow, he added, "I think I have an idea, but the point is you keep pushing it, and..." J. J. let the statement hang.

With penetrating eyes, Zadok answered. "Yes. It is worth dying for."

Looking away, he added, "My daddy died standing up for himself; I will too, if I have to."

The lawman folded his arms over his chest. "And is your family ready to lose you?"

Silently, the black man scowled.

Then J.J. sighed. "Well, do what you have to do." He glanced about. "I'll do what I can, but you know I'm limited here."

"I know. And I appreciate it. I appreciate what you have already done for me."

The deputy smirked. "Hell, all I did was let you out of jail."

Zadok argued. "You went and talked to that moonshiner!"

His companion scoffed. "You already uncovered that information!"

The black man smiled. "It's the thought that counts."

Leading his companion, down the walk the deputy ignored the curious stares of the folks on the street.

"So now you will go to Almaville."

"Yes."

"When?"

"When does the next bus for Alamville leave town?"

Hesitating, J.J. frowned. "Why?" He looked up and down the street. "Where's your pickup?"

"It's at Doc Orley's place."

"Doc Orley's! Why?"

Zadok explained the whole episode, from the incident at the gas station to pushing the truck into the physician's garage.

"So you're gonna take the bus, huh?"

"Yes."

"Well, the bus leaves at 6:45. It's..." he checked his watch, "just after 7:00 now!" Frowning, the lawman glanced about. "So do you want a ride home? I can pick you up sometime tomorrow afternoon."

Zadok shook his head. "No, I want to stay in town."

"Stay where?"

The black man shrugged. "I don't know. Maybe I'll find some place in Darky Town."

J.J. tapped the back of his hand against his companion's chest. "Why don't you stay at my place tonight? I'm going to spend the night at Liddy Mae's place anyway."

Zadok wrinkled his nose. "I don't know."

"Look," the lawman contended, "you gotta sleep somewhere. I'll be gone the whole night. Help yourself to some grub. Make yourself at home. You'll have the whole place to yourself—well, you and Buster—he's my dog." J.J. grinned. "You can watch TV, or listen to the radio, to help pass the time."

With an approving smile, the black man raised his brows. "That does sound good."

Returning the smile, the pleased deputy, once again, tapped his companion's chest. "Then it's settled."

And, without a thought, he threw his arm over Zadok's shoulder.

Zadok stood at the kitchen window with a cup of coffee in his hand, gazing into the big backyard. He hated the inactivity, the waiting. But he did appreciate that J.J. let him stay at the house. The night before, television had distracted him from his pressing concerns. But when the station signed off, Zadok had tossed and turned while lying on the sofa. He knew that it was in the wee hours of the morning, before he finally drifted off to sleep. Even then, the man had woken up from his light sleep several times. It was eight o'clock in the morning when Zadok gave up and rose from the sofa.

For the next several hours, the man had found chores to keep him busy. Though his host had offered him the use of his kitchen, and his choice of the fare, Zadok only helped himself to coffee. And he didn't disturb the contents of the house. After brewing the coffee, the man had settled on the sofa and listened to the radio. Then he had spent some time playing with the deputy's brown stocky mutt in the backyard. Zadok then decided to re-stack the firewood and pick up the few scattered items strewn in the yard by the dog. After pulling weeds from around the house, the guest was idle again.

And that was when he found himself staring out of the kitchen window. The man felt as though he would bust. He considered walking into town, as J.J.'s place was only about a mile and a half distance from there.

Decisively, Zadok poured out the rest of his coffee into the sink, rinsed out his cup, and left the house. As it was nearly four in the afternoon, the sun seemed to stare down on the man, while he plodded down Blue Oak St., a road that laid between large parcels of farmland and few homes. Turning south on Blue Jay Rd., the pedestrian could see the schoolhouse on the edge of town. Just before Zadok passed the school, he spied the patrol car headed his way. The cruiser screeched to a halt, beside him, and the lawman popped out of the cab.

Frowning, J.J. demanded, "What are you doing? I told you I would pick you up!"

"I got antsy." The black man grunted.

His companion sighed. "Well, get in."

As the two rode into town, J.J. stated, "I figured I would come get you after my afternoon rounds. How was the stay at the house?"

"Fine. Thank you, for that."

"You're welcome."

After a brief pause, the deputy added, "Well, you still have about two hours before the bus leaves. I'll get us some supper from the burger stand and bring it over to the office."

"I'm not hungry."

The driver turned to Zadok. "Not hungry? You eat anything over at the house?"

"I just had coffee. My stomach was flitting."

"Nerves?" J.J. gave a half-smile. "That's fine. But I'm going to buy you a burger, and you're going to eat something, before you leave town."

Dropping his passenger off in front of the sheriff's office, the lawman drove off. Zadok went inside. He sat at the desk, in line with the current of rushing air being churned by the fan that sat on the cabinet. The man closed his eyes and basked in the refreshing breeze.

Leaning on his elbows atop the desk, Zadok's foot twitched. He was full of nervous energy. Doubts began to invade his mind. What would he accomplish besides getting himself killed? Would he be stopped before he could even find the perpetrators, before he could exact his vengeance? Would he panic and freeze, rather than act? With a shake of his head, the man pushed the doubts from his mind. Though stressed and weary, Zadok would not allow his resolve to dissipate. Rising to his feet, the man began to pace and fidget.

J. J. walked through the door, clutching two white sacks and paused as he noticed his companion's tense demeanor. "I hope you like barbecue sauce."

Crossing the room, the deputy sat the sacks on the desk. "What's wrong?"

Zadok shrugged. "Just antsy."

J.J. pushed a bag towards the black man. "Well, here. Eat."

Reluctantly, Zadok hesitated, before slowly opening the sack and taking out a bottle of Coca-Cola and a wrapped burger. Like Pavlov's dog, the man's hunger was triggered by the aroma of the fare. The lawman popped the caps from the bottles with an opener hanging from his key chain. He handed one of the bottles to his companion. Thanking the deputy, Zadok drank half of the bottle's contents before sinking his teeth into the burger. He relished the mouthful of flavor.

J.J. took a deep swig from his bottle before stating, "I'd try to talk you out of this notion, but I think you've come too far to decide to turn back now." He studied the anxious man. "Or have you?"

Zadok pushed away the recollection of his recent uncertainty. "I have." He grunted.

Taking another bite of the burger, the black man drained the Coke bottle. He banged the empty vessel on the desk top.

Then Zadok strode to the door. "I'm going to go buy my ticket."

Wide-eyed, the lawman stared after him.

Walking up Main Street, Zadok crossed the road to the bus depot that adjoined the gas station. He entered the white-washed concrete building. Bright colored, plastic Eiffel chairs sat against the front wall. Before the counter, two customers stood in tandem. The white-haired woman behind the counter smiled most cordially, her slack jowls rising at the patrons, and her blue eyes sparkled as she served each in turn.

Then Zadok stepped up to the counter. The clerk's pleasant countenance instantly transformed; her forehead furrowed and shadowed her scowling eyes. Her jowls sagged, as her smile sank to a loathing frown. Then the woman looked past Zadok and waved the next customer, standing behind the black man, forward. The white man pushed past Zadok. Though she didn't smile, the clerk's face softened, while she politely served the customer.

After the patron walked away, Zadok, once again, stepped up to the counter. The woman's expression of disdain returned. The abrupt transformations were almost startling.

She harshly demanded, "What you want, boy?"

The black man felt his stomach flutter. But he looked her in the glowering eyes and met her vile grimace. "I would like a ticket to Almaville."

Like a gargoyle, she was still. Then, in exasperation, the woman goaded, "Well, one way or round trip?" After a fraction of a moment, the woman snapped at the contemplating customer. "One way or round trip? Which is it, jig?"

Zadok arched a brow over his level eyes. "One way."

Again, she glared with utter contempt, before she badgered on, "You got the money?"

"I believe so. How much will that cost?"

Like an overheated radiator, the clerk hissed out a sigh. Zadok imagined her head bursting and blasting steam. "Three, twenty-five"

Taking his worn wallet from his hip pocket, the man began sifting through bills.

"Hurry up!" the clerk snapped.

Zadok paused and, while peering at her, laid the fourth dollar bill on the counter. Like a striking snake, the woman slapped her spotted wrinkled hand onto the cash, and snatched the bills into the cash drawer. Then, she took a ticket, slashed her pen across it, and slapped the voucher on the counter.

Picking up the ticket, Zadok eyed the old woman as if she were crazy. He expectantly waited for his change.

The clerk suddenly barked. "Well, move on, nigger!"

"What about my change?"

"Outta quarters! Move on, nigger!"

The man deliberately fixed a patronizing look on his face. "Thank you, ma'am"

Incredibly, her visage puckered all the more. Turning away, Zadok couldn't help but smile to himself. He walked over and sat in the end chair, away from the seated white patrons.

In a fury, the clerk leaned over the counter, her gnarled hands like a vulture's talons clutching the edge, and bellowed. "You can't sit there, you ignorant dumb nigger! Those chairs are for decent white folks! Niggers wait outside!"

Incredulous, Zadok stared at the enraged woman. A defiant notion flashed in his mind.

"Move, boy!"

The resentful black man slowly rose to his feet and ambled out of the door. Beside the depot was a lean-to comprised of weathered gray timber. Two black people sat on the bench, an old two-by-eight spanning the back wall of the crude shelter, a woman donned in a brown print dress, whom Zadok judged to be in her fifties, and a slim man wearing a gray jacket and a bow tie, whom Zadok presumed was no older than seventy. He nodded to the seated patrons and stepped just under the lean-to, in order to get out of the sun.

He inquired of the two, "Headed for Alamville?"

The woman smiled and nodded.

"Jacinda," the elderly man replied.

Raising his brows, Zadok commented, "You have a ways to go!"

The man smiled and nodded.

The three introduced themselves to one another and engaged in small talk, until the bus pulled into the depot. Standing, the elderly man waited for the woman to rise and lead the way to the bus. Zadok brought up the rear. They stood aside, while the white boarders lined up, then the trio filed behind them. As the white riders filled the forward seats, the black riders made their way to the back. Zadok sat alone and stared out of the window.

The bus pulled out of the depot. Zadok tried to focus on the scenery rather than on his mission. The bus drove past Darky Town, a collective of crowded shanties, hovels, and lean-tos, a depressing sight. And the man was grateful that his family didn't have to reside there with the glum and humble Negroes, whom he pitied. The man felt separate from those who lived there, but not superior. And yet, maybe he did feel superior.

Maybe he was being punished for his hubris. Could God be punishing his wife and son, as well? Tassy, who always gave what she could to those in need, filled with compassion and empathy, Gideon, who had a gentle spirit? The injustice angered him.

Shaking the thoughts from his head, Zadok gazed out at the changing countryside: Canby's dairy, Packard's mules, and Sample's hogs, Henshaw's peas and green beans, Anderson's cotton, and Kendall's beef cattle. The bus turned left onto a junction of highway and skirted Pettyjohn's cornfield and Tibbideau's sweet potatoes. Zadok looked over Campbell's orchards. He looked across the aisle, out of the far window, onto Baird's peanut farm, where he had been working the night his family was assaulted. The dreadful thought had returned to haunt his mind.

Zadok began to wonder why he couldn't be somebody else. Why did he have to be colored, or better yet, why did colored folk have to suffer so? Other than the condescending treatment he had received at times, Zadok liked being black; he was proud of who he was and from where he came. In the mornings, before work, he would look in the mirror and was pleased with his reflection, his handsome features—his square chin and tapering jawline, his prominent cheek bones, inherent of his Cherokee bloodline. The man's thick brows arced over dark confident eyes. His wide nose and full mouth were not so large as to dominate his face. Zadok liked his smooth chestnut brown skin and the swell of his muscles beneath his flesh. He was long of limb, tall, and broad.

And he loved who his wife was. The man considered her the most beautiful woman he had ever seen. They called her "high-yeller", but her smooth skin was a lovely golden brown tone. Her wavy thick hair was raven black and cascaded over her shoulders, like a rolling waterfall. Tassy's almond eyes had a sparkle that reflected her wonderful spirit, as did her gleaming smile. He recalled her button nose and her shapely lips fixed in her heart-shaped face.

In his mind's eye, Zadok pictured her stepping out of the shower, and imagined her golden brown skin shimmering, her curving figure—firm breasts, round hips, long shapely limbs.

"And to think," he muttered to himself, "her color and her beauty are what led to her rape."

He longed for the time when she would once again welcome his touch. He wanted to feel her soft smooth flesh under his caressing hands, embrace her body and feel her warmth, kiss her beautiful face, her soft tender lips. Zadok couldn't imagine changing a thing about his wife. Even twenty-two years after he'd first seen her, Tassy was just as beautiful, though her beauty was enhanced with her maturity. She had bloomed, rather than withered.

Then, the husband began to wonder if he would ever see his wife again.

Zadok pictured images, in his mind, of the three assailants. He figured they would be around Bernie Stover's age, young men, in their late teens or early twenties. But he imagined them to be hulking brutish characters, small ugly headed ogres, with massive hunched shoulders and barreled chests, thick torsos, long apish arms and short bowed legs.

Of course, Zadok knew that the images he had concocted were unrealistic. But, he wondered what were the assailants like? The black man wasn't a fighter. As an adult, he had never struck another person in anger. Would he be able to vindicate his family, or would he lend to their shame? Would he be adding fuel to the fire of hate and cruelty?

Once more, Zadok peered out of the window, trying to dissipate his discouraging thoughts, while gazing over the timberland and meadows. But he couldn't help wondering why colored folk were destined to such adversity? Some claimed that black skin was the cursed mark of Cain. But the man knew that to be foolishness. Noah was a direct descendant of Adam's son, Seth. And only Noah and his family, his wife, his sons, and their wives survived the flood. The descendants of Cain were destroyed, unless one of Noah's sons had married a black-skinned daughter of Cain. And if that had been the case, what would that say about inequality, about racial purity?

Were there any other reasons that might justify the suffering of the black race at the hands of their white counterparts? Zadok couldn't think of any.

Tassy was wringing out laundry when her mother-in-law entered the utility room. She didn't look up; Tassy knew what the old woman would say—"I told you not to bother with that laundry."

But instead, Mother Quarry growled. "That husband of yours..."

With a jolt, the wife jerked herself upright and turned, finding the old woman scowling, leaning against a table, with her arms folded over her breasts.

"What?" Tassy desperately implored.

Her mother-in-law looked like a simmering pot about to boil over. "That boy, of... He- I just finished talking on the phone, with Regina! She said Zadok had gone to that klansman's barber shop and cut his throat, with a razor!"

Tassy covered her gaping mouth with her hand as she gasped. She pressed the damp towel she was clutching in her other hand against her breast, while her heart pounded.

"Is he alright?"

With a dismissive turn of her head, Mother Quarry assured her, "Yes. It wasn't more than a flesh wound."

Tassy cried, "I was asking about Zadok!"

"Oh! Yes. The deputy came and took him in. But after he's let go, Zadok goes up to the house! And that same night, the Klan goes up there!"

The wife slumped. One hand, once more, covered her mouth, while the other pressed against her stomach. Her mother-in-law stepped forward and grasped her shoulders.

"Easy, girl! Zadok was unharmed, but that Royal fella was nearly burned to death. Somehow, he caught his sheet on fire! Regina said something about fire from heaven! She said it was some kind of miracle, that God was watching out for him!"

Tassy had slid down the washer and sat with her knees drawn. "Oh God, I hope so."

The old woman had descended with her daughter-in-law and knelt in front of her. "Well, Regina said that he and that deputy had been seen around town, hanging on each other, like life long pals!"

Puzzled, Tassy frowned.

Mother Quarry pursed her mouth. "And Regina said he was seen getting on the bus!"

"What?" The wife knitted her brows. "Where to?"

Her mother-in-law shrugged. "Regina doesn't know."

Looking as though she were enduring a sudden pang, Tassy furrowed her brow. "Is he running away? Is he leaving us?"

She slumped her head to the back of her hand, which, laying on top of the other, rested on her knee. Mother Quarry rubbed her shoulder.

"No, my boy isn't running away. He wouldn't leave without coming here for you and Giddy. Unless..."

Tassy looked up. "Unless what?"

"Well, unless they were after him; unless he had to stay away to keep you and Giddy safe."

Wrapping her arms about her stomach, the wife looked up to the ceiling, her eyes welling and her lip quivering. Mother Quarry embraced her.

As the bus decelerated, Zadok noticed a market and gas station up ahead. Pulling into the parking lot, the driver braked, and the bus hissed to a stop.

He turned in his seat, and addressed the passengers. "Folks, we'll be loading some cargo here. It will be about twenty minutes, so go ahead and stretch, use the restrooms, and go buy some refreshments from the market."

As the riders disembarked, the driver cordially smiled. Then the black woman stepped into the aisle and started forward. Zadok followed. They had nearly reached the door when the driver jerked the lever and slammed the door shut with a whoosh.

Glaring, he snapped at the two, "Ya'll go back to your seats!"

The black woman pleaded, "Please, sir, I need to use the restroom."

"Well, why the hell didn't you go, before we boarded?" he scolded her. "I'm not gonna end up havin' to round you niggers up, to get back on the bus, come time to leave! So sit back down!"

When the woman turned to comply, Zadok saw her despondent eyes and humiliated frown. He felt his ire rise, as he slipped past the dejected woman and stepped up to the driver. His expression was placid, as he looked down on the man.

Zadok's voice started low and quiet but gradually gained volume, as he argued. "Now look here, it isn't going to hurt to let us off of the bus; we can tell time, just like those white folks out there. When you call the riders to board, we can hear and understand, just as good as those white folks can." His face transformed into a hard scowl; his voice had escalated, to a near roar. "So open the damn door!"

The driver's eyes reflected a mixture of anger and intimidation. His face paled. His body tensed. His eyes lost their edge, as he fixed on the black man's stern glare. Slowly, he pushed the lever, opening the door. Zadok stepped down from the bus, then took the hesitant black woman's arm, assisting her down the step. Then the man leaned on the near by gas pump. He watched the woman make her way to the side of the station. Facing the building, she halted. Then, apparently reading a sign that stated, "Whites only," she slumped her shoulders. Evidently, there were no facilities provided for colored people.

The black woman turned her head towards timber, behind the station. Zadok surmised that she was considering her only other option. Then, a young white woman emerged from the bathroom and was given a start as she confronted the anxious black woman. For a moment, their eyes locked. Then, the young woman glanced from side to side. With a furtive wave of her hand, she beckoned the black woman, who was hesitant. But the conspirator was insistent. Summoning her resolve, the black woman entered. After it closed, the white woman stood next to the door, as if guarding a post.

Impressed, Zadok approached. He stood several feet in front of the woman and, when their eyes met, gave an appreciative nod.

The woman quickly diverted her eyes. She reminded the man of a nervous hen. But she was taking a risk, defying the Jim Crow rules of an ignorant and hateful culture. Zadok was pleased to find another reasonable and compassionate person among this society.

He returned to the pump. With hands in pockets, he waited until the driver climbed back onto the bus, and the passengers lined up to reboard. Zadok stepped to the back of the line, behind the black woman. He was yet delighting in the recollection of the young white woman's kind deed, and in the black woman's relief.

The white riders had all boarded. The black woman stepped onto the bus. As soon as she cleared the door, and as Zadok was preparing to step up, the door, with a squeal and a rattle, snapped shut. The driver gave the black man a smug glare. Then he pulled the bus away.

Cursing under his breath, Zadok glowered at the passing windows, from which a few white faces, with looks of disdain or indifference, met his glare. He stared after the receding bus and, from the back window, saw two black faces sympathetically frowning back at him with doleful eyes. For a moment, he felt more sorrow for them than he did for himself. With a resigned smile, Zadok shrugged, then waved to the glum pair.

He watched the vehicle disappear into the distance and found himself gazing down an empty road. Uncertain, the man stood. It would be dark by the time he reached Almaville, on foot. And, if he were to turn back, he would have a longer journey to return home. The man contemplated. Should he press on or relent? Zadok had come this far, but he yet had a long way to go. So many obstacles had stood before the man, though he had overcome them. But he was growing weary and discouraged.

Would it be best to let this obsession go? With a sigh, Zadok hung his head.

Then, the man summoned his resolve. It would be worth the demanding effort; it would be worth the costly toll. It would be worth dying for. This was for his family, for their vindication, their declaration of worth. He would push on into the uncertainty. He would face all future obstacles, with determination and courage. Zadok would not be deterred, unless he was utterly overcome or dead.

Like a rooster about to crow, the man expanded his chest, then, with newfound resolve, blew out his breath. "Well, better get started."

Drawing back his shoulders, Zadok proceeded. He trudged past cotton fields, tobacco and sorghum fields, before the man came to a black willow tree beside the road. By that time, he had covered about five miles, and his stomach was growling. Other than a couple of bites from a burger, Zadok hadn't eaten since he sat with J.J. at his kitchen table and shared half of a strawberry-rhubarb pie with the lawman. His mouth was dry. The man's body was damp and sticky with the sweat that soaked his clothing. Zadok's legs ached; his feet were sore.

So, beneath the boughs of the black willow, the traveler stiffly lowered himself to his knees and sat back on his rear. Removing his boots, Zadok wiggled his toes. His feet throbbed. The man wondered if it was wise to sit and rest. He feared that it would be harder to start again, after his body had cooled and stiffened, rather than to have just kept going. But the weary hiker was seated with his aching back against the hard rough tree trunk. He closed his eyes, as the setting sun seemed to stare in his face. And he actually drifted off into a semi-conscious sleep. With a start, Zadok awoke. Shaking his head, the man peered towards the horizon. The man hadn't slept long, for the rim of the sun could still be seen, edging the tops of the distant wood. A bank of dark clouds were drifting in from the south. His stiff back throbbed, as Zadok reached for his boots and slipped them back onto his sore feet. Pushing off of the tree trunk, the pedestrian stood. He stretched his arms and flexed his legs. Dull pain radiated throughout his body as he "worked out the kinks." Glumly, Zadok looked down the road. It seemed an endless stretch of pavement. The man had a few more miles to go. So, wearily, he trudged up to the shoulder of the highway and plodded on.

The driver sped his two-toned '57 Chevy Bel Air down the road. Tapping his fingers on the steering wheel, he listened to "Volare" play on the radio. The man gazed through the windshield, into the twilight, and fidgeted in the seat. He ran his hand through his strawberry blonde hair. The long drive had grown monotonous. Then the driver spotted a man tramping along the road, a Negro, he realized as he drew nearer. The redhead was tired and bored. Perhaps the colored man would serve as a distraction for a while. Pulling up along-side of the pedestrian, the driver hollered through the open window.

"Need a lift?" He displayed a white smile.

The black man warily approached the passenger's door and scrutinized the white man.

"I'm headed for Almaville," Zadok stated.

"I'm thinkin' about stoppin' there for the night myself," the driver replied. "If you want a lift..."

Peering through the window, the black man seemed to be assessing the situation. Then, he decisively opened the door and dropped into the set.

"I appreciate it, sir," Zadok muttered.

As the driver accelerated up the highway, he commented, "Never picked up a Negro before." He glanced over at the big brooding man. "I'm from Brownsburg, myself, up north—not many Negroes in that neck of the woods."

The passenger silently stared out of the side window.

The driver persisted, "Name's Russell, Allan Russell. I'm a salesman—novelties: key chains, lighters, pens, wall magnets. I have new clients in Tanouye."

"Zadok Quarry," the black man muttered, while still turned to the side window.

For a few moments, the two rode in silence.

Then, licking his lips, Allan brazenly asked, "You ever have a white woman, Zadok?"

He glanced over to his passenger, who, with an incredulous scowl, looked back, obviously thinking his host's inquiry absurd.

Emphatically, the black man answered, "No!"

The salesman grinned. "I bet you've had plenty of colored gals, though, huh?"

Zadok silently stared out of the windshield.

Allan explained, "I ask because I have acquaintances who travel the South a lot, and they tell me that colored girls are real lusty! You know? They really get into it!" He shot a lecherous grin to his passenger. "You know what I mean?"

Getting no response, the driver pressed on, "A few of 'em even had colored girls before, and they say it was the best sex that they ever had!"

The black man seemed to be ignoring him, and Allan was getting offended. The Negro was lucky to be getting a ride, from a white man, in this part of the country. Yet, the colored man seemed rude and unappreciative.

"Well, come on, boy!" the salesman prodded. "You aren't a virgin, are you?"

"No," Zadok muttered. "I'm married."

"Oh," Allan gave a hopeful smile, "so you've been with women!"

Turning his glaring eyes on his host, Zadok rasped, "I've been with one woman, my wife. I've been with her, and only her, going on twenty-one years now."

The driver grinned, as he stared, wide-eyed, out of the windshield. "I heard colored girls get like Holy Rollers at a prayer meeting when they're in the sack, thrashing and flopping about, and hollering, just like they'd been slain in the spirit!"

"I can only speak for my wife." Zadok interjected. "She and I do enjoy one another. And she is a passionate woman. But she hardly thrashes and flops about, or hollers."

Feeling discouraged, Allan fell silent. For a time, only the drone of the engine and Pat Boone crooning, "Ain't that a Shame" could be heard.

Then Zadok appended, "I've heard the same reports about colored people; we hop from one bed to another, we're lusty and shameless, like animals, we all want a white woman, or a white man."

Pausing, the black man contemplated, while gazing into space. Then he continued, "I suppose there is some truth to those accusations. I've wondered about it. And I've wondered why that would be so." He looked over to his host. "You know, maybe some colored folk use sex as an escape, a distraction, from the dreariness and hopelessness in their lives. Maybe they use sex to prove themselves; maybe it's the only time a colored man can feel like a real man, and the only time a colored woman can feel like a real woman."

Allan fidgeted uncomfortably, while his passenger went on, "The colored live in poverty, with no hope of getting out. They are looked down upon and subjected to disdain. The white folk call them 'boy' or 'girl', and won't even acknowledge them as men or as women. And they even call them worse—no good, no account. And the colored become what they are labeled, because they aren't allowed to better themselves. So, I suppose they turn to sex, in order to validate themselves, their masculinity, their femininity, their humanity."

Zadok sighed. "Maybe they figure that the more people with whom they have sex, the more their masculinity, their femininity, or their humanity is proven. That would explain promiscuous behavior. They need that reassurance."

He shifted in his seat. "The ones that find jobs, break their backs, then take their meager pay home to their shanties, scraping to keep enough food on the table, to keep raggedy clothes on their children's back and, maybe, shabby shoes on their feet. And after a meager meal, they sit on their stoops, feeling lowly and pathetic.

"So they hide in the dark, and hold one another, dismissing the outside world, the hardships and woes, finding physical and emotional release with their intimate embraces. And, maybe, in their attempt to smother the hardships and woes, they exaggerate their passion, embellish their lust."

Impressed with his passenger, Allan ventured, "But you don't seem that way—I mean you don't seem lowly or dispirited."

The black man grinned. "Well, when a fisherman casts his net and makes an abundant catch, he doesn't worry about the few that got away. I reckon I get away with living better than most colored, and get away with being proud and dignified, because there are plenty for the white folk to subject to oppression and humiliation. They have plenty of darkies to kick about."

The salesman gained respect for his rider. The man was intelligent, articulate, not the "Stepin Fetchit" type, of whom he came to expect, the type of whom he had constantly heard.

Zadok continued, "As for wanting white sex partners, that may be a desire to uplift oneself to a higher status. Perhaps some Negroes feel less inferior should they be accepted by a white sex partner. Maybe they gain a misplaced feeling of acceptance, though I myself don't know of any colored man who would ever risk having sex with a white woman. Just looking at a white woman can get a Negro killed!"

He looked to Allan. "You ever hear about Emmett Till? A few years back, the fourteen-year-old colored boy went down to Mississippi, to visit his uncle. He was standing outside a shop, with some local kids, and, on a dare, Emmett went inside the store, whistled at the white cashier, and called her 'baby'. And for that, he was taken from his uncle's house, beaten, and killed. A fourteen-year-old boy."

The passenger glared through the windshield. "As for the colored girls I've heard about who sleep with white men, do it for money and gifts—and perhaps, in some cases, for that feeling of acceptance. But they are whores—not because they are full of lust, but because they are full of need; they need the money to feed their children, to pay the rent."

Zadok sighed. "I don't mean to make out that all colored folk would be perfect, if not for their oppression, or that all white folk are villains. There are good and bad in both races, in all races. I know plenty of decent white folk. But, as for me, I never have desired a white woman, or any woman, other than my wife."

Then, with a boastful smile and raised brows, the black man sat up. "But my wife has been with a white man!"

Allan gaped. The boast and sudden change in demeanor baffled him. But his interest was renewed.

"Yeah," Zadok exclaimed, "in fact, she was with two men at one time!" His mock boasting gave way to a grim visage. "It wasn't by choice, though. No, these men forced their way into our house. They beat my son and raped my wife, while I was away, working."

Closing his gaping mouth, the driver swallowed, and stared out of the windshield, into the night. An awkward silence followed.

Finally, the passenger spoke, "Look, just pull over, and I'll walk the rest of the way."

"No!" Allan blurted. "I'll drive you the rest of the way!"

Zadok fixed his host with an uncertain look.

"No, really!" The driver glanced at the odometer. "We've only got about two miles to go!"

With his eyes, the passenger assented.

Then, the driver apologized, "I'm sorry. I didn't know." With a deep sigh, he went on to explain, "Look, all I know about Negroes is what I've heard from acquaintances, and, evidently, most of that is bullshit. I guess—well, I did think Negroes were different, not as smart, not as—well, I don't know—human, maybe. Well, I just didn't know."

Zadok's frown faded, as he nodded. Gazing out of the window, the black man mused, "We may look different, but we're just a different shade, with slight differences in our features. But inside, we are all the same. Our blood runs red. We all have brains, hearts, and lungs. We all experience love, hate, joy, despair, fear, and pain."

Zadok ended his discourse with Sammy Kaye's, "It isn't Fair", playing on the radio.

As the Chevy sped on, a dilapidated gray barn sitting in the midst of a field, just outside of town, came into sight. And just beyond the weathered building stood a sign at the edge of the highway that read, "Welcome to Almaville". Proceeding along the main street of town, the Chevy approached a burger stand on the right hand side.

"Let me buy you a burger!" Allan offered his passenger.

He noticed a glint in Zadok's eye.

But the black man answered, "I can't go in there; I'm not allowed."

The driver persisted, "I'll park at the edge of the parking lot, and I'll bring the food out to the car."

The salesman noticed the glimpse of hope in his passenger's face.

And Zadok assented. "Alright. I could use a bite."

Allan pulled the Chevy into the driveway. There were a few

cars parked around the restaurant. The salesman parked in the dark far corner of the lot and walked over to the building. Though his conversation with his passenger hadn't gone as he anticipated, Allan felt all the wiser. And it pleased him to be helping out this particular fellow.

He stood outside of the window and placed his order, then leaned against the ledge while he waited. When his order was up, the customer carried the sacks of burgers, fries, and drinks to his car. He noticed Zadok's anticipation as he handed a sack to the black man through the open window.

Settling in the seat, Allan joined his companion. They consumed their burgers and fries, and gulped their drinks in the quiet.

While the salesman wadded up wrappers and stuffed them in a sack, Zadok said, "Well, I'd better go and tend to my business."

"Anywhere I can drop you?"

With an appreciative grin, the black man replied, "No. I'm not really sure where I'm going."

He opened the car door, and Allan offered his hand. "Hey, it was nice meeting you! Good luck!"

A smile slowly crossed his face, as Zadok took the salesman hand. "Thank you."

Impressed with, and awed by, the character of the man, qualities he hadn't expected to find in a Negro, Allan lingered on the man's broad back, while Zadok made his way across the parking lot, towards the street.

Shaking his head, the salesman said to himself, "Live and learn."

Reaching the lamp-lit sidewalk, Zadok walked to the corner and crossed to the next block. As he ambled along, the man searched the facades of buildings, looking for a sign that denoted "Stucky's Pool Hall". Zadok had nearly reached the next corner when he found a white teenaged boy sitting on the curb.

Excuse me, son," he addressed the boy, who turned to the voice, looking up and wrinkling his nose, "Do you know Monty Dinmont, Reggie Brisby or Arvis Shelley?"

"Yep," the boy casually replied. "I know 'em all."

"Would you know where I could find them?"

Looking up the road, the teenager gave a nod. "Prob'ly over at Stucky's. 'less Monty's joy ridin' in his Buick."

"Where is Stucky's?"

The boy gave a more specific indication and pointed across the road towards the next block over. "Over there."

"Thank you." Zadok gave the teenager a grateful nod.

Jogging across the main street, the black man strode along the walk. His stomach felt heavy and knotted. Perhaps he had eaten too much on a nervous empty stomach. But at least he didn't feel as fatigued, as he had before the ride and the meal. He was yet somewhat stiff and sore.

He came to a lettered window, proclaiming, "Stucky's Pool Hall, Pinball & Refreshments". Taking a deep, uneasy breath, the man pushed the air through his puckered lips. His stomach fluttered.

It was one thing to undergo the long taxing journey, but now that he had arrived, it was another thing to finally come face to face with the uncertain danger. And Zadok knew that the odds were overwhelmingly against him. Standing before the entrance, the man, once again, questioned his actions. But, once again, he dismissed his doubts and fears, determined to face opposition, no matter how futile it seemed.

Nervously, Zadok opened the door and stepped into the dim entry. To his right stood a counter surrounded by the walls of an office. A tough looking fellow with stubble, wearing a t-shirt and red cap, chewing on a stubby cigar, leaned, braced on his elbows, on the counter top. Hooded by the bill of his cap, the proprietor's stern eyes seemed to size up the black man.

"You lost, boy?" he challenged through clenched teeth.

"No, sir," Zadok, standing before the counter, humbly answered. "I'm looking for Monty Dinmont, Reggie..."

"Hey, Mutt!" the other interrupted and hollered into the hall beyond. "There's a darkie here lookin' for ya!"

Peering into the hall, Zadok saw a group gathered about one of the pool tables.

He spotted the black and tan jacket, emblazoned with a red razorback, before the young man turned and replied, "A darkie? What's he want?"

"I dunno!" The proprietor sounded perturbed. "Come ask 'im yourself!"

"Send him in!"

"You know I don' let coons into my place!"

"Ah, come on, Stucky! Just this once!"

Turning on the black man with a scowl, the proprietor gave a harsh nod towards the hall. Zadok hesitated. He anxiously studied the patrons. Besides the group that included Monty, there was a couple of young men at another pool table, three young fellows standing before a pinball machine, while others stood, observing, along the walls. All eyes had turned, and suspiciously stared at the black man, as he warily approached Monty and his clique.

Two fresh-faced girls mingled with the three young men; one, a tall slim blonde, donned in a tight pink sweater and a pair of pale blue culottes, arched a brow and gave a lurid smile. She seemed to carnally appraise the tall, broad, and handsome black man. Zadok dismissed the leering blonde and focused his attention on the boys. Monty was as tall, and perhaps as broad, as was the black man, an athletic type, probably a football or wrestling star. His fresh handsome face expressed a cocky self-assurance, and his blue eyes had a sinister glint.

Zadok could guess who the other two young men were. He recognized Monty's co-conspirators from the descriptions given by his family. A slim brunette sat on the corner of the pool table, with an arrogant smirk. The short sleeves of his striped t-shirt were rolled up above his long tanned arms. And the boy standing on the other side of the table wore a baggy, plaid, short-sleeved shirt and tan trousers. Clasping his right arm with his left hand, the boy was quiet and seemed timid. A wisp of chestnut hair drooped down his forehead, nearly reaching his dull eyes.

Monty's mouth turned with a half-smile when, leaning on his pool cue he faced the black man.

"You're a big buck, ain't ya?"

Zadok's fists clinched. A surge of fury washed through him as he faced the villains who had violated his family. Their smug behavior caused his heart to pound and his body trembled, like an overheated boiler about to blow.

Monty went on, "I bet I know who you are and why you're here."

He slightly cocked his head towards Reggie, but kept his eye on the black man. "What do you think, Reg? You think this is that high-yeller bitch's man, the big buck nigger Bernie was tellin' us about?"

"I bet it is." Reggie's hardened eyes narrowed.

"What do you want, boy?" Monty demanded. "Your little woman askin' after us?"

There were snickers about the table.

Glaring into the young man's smug face, Zadok curled his lip. "Seems you do know who I am and why I'm here," he rasped. "There's that old barn on the edge of town. I'll be waiting there for the three of you."

In turn, Zadok fixed his smoldering eyes on each member of the trio. Monty's amused smirk didn't alter. But Reggie's scowling face grew more taut. Arvis seemed to pale.

"I'll be there." Monty grinned. Again, his head slightly cocked towards his cohorts, while his eyes remained on Zadok. "Reg, Arvy?"

"We'll be there," Reggie asserted.

Arvis remained silent, his face expressing his uncertainty.

Turning on his heel, Zadok strode towards the door, while the patrons let out facetious ooh's and ah's.

When the black man neared the counter, Stucky frowned as he leaned over the counter. "You're one crazy coon! They're gonna kill ya!"

In passing, Zadok glowered, "It'll be one less nigger, huh."

He slammed the door as he walked out. Shoulders tense, the man shoved his hands in his pockets and controlled himself from hyperventilating. He could feel his body shake and his knees weaken. Zadok almost felt faint. With halting breaths, the man looked up to the nearly full moon. As the orb rose, it would soon be immersed into the dark clouds above. The air about him was growing muggy.

The black man pulled back his shoulders, took a deep breath, and pushed it out, then, resolutely, started down the main street. While he walked through the quiet town, he noticed that the boy, who had been sitting on the curb, was gone. Oddly, Zadok felt abandoned, his solitude compounded.

Near the city limits, the lone man crossed the street and trudged past the Almaville welcome sign. The concrete walk ended. Zadok stepped onto the shoulder of the road and skittered down the slope that swept down to the field holding the barn.

Filtered with dim moonlight, the meadow appeared olive gray. The black man stood before the dilapidated barn with its sagging door and gaping weather-worn vertical planking. He found several split shingles and splintered chunks of wood littering the ground about the run-down structure.

The door creaking, in protest, on its ancient hinges, Zadok slowly pushed it open and stepped inside the gloom. He surveyed the interior. The round moon peeking through the cloud cover provided a dim, dusky silver light that shone through the gaps in the planking, casting shadows like long narrow blades of a gigantic harrow. Busted boards and chunks of wood cluttered the flaky dusty floor. The pungent odor of ancient dung and moldered straw faintly hung about the airy building.

Zadok imagined other scents. The odors of the sweat and dried blood of colored people who had been tortured and killed in this structure by arrogant klansmen, the stench of whose remnant hate and fear seemed to permeate throughout the barn, lingering and haunting the atmosphere. A few precarious beams supported the warped frame. Next to one of the beams was an overturned steel tub. The man walked over to the tub and sat, hunched over, with his elbows resting, on his knees.

He gazed over the strange patterns made by shafts of light and bars of shadow, considering the history of the old barn. It had been built almost one hundred years ago for housing livestock and storing feed. But the Great Depression hit. The Stroop family lost the farm, and the structure was adopted as a meeting place, a klavern, by the local chapter of klansmen. Then, it more or less became a torture chamber, where uppity niggers were brought for punishment—whippings, beatings, flayings, acid baths, castrations, lynchings and burnings.

And Zadok would, most likely, become the infamous structure's next victim, though the black man had come of his own volition; he wasn't dragged to the barn, kicking and pleading. But Zadok intended, if he could, to put up one hell of a fight. He feared that they might shoot him before he could even begin to act. It could be over that fast. He had no idea of what was to come. And the man had never been so anxious and nervous in his life. His fantasy of finding his family's attackers and dealing with them was becoming a reality. Zadok was in the middle of it now.

While he contemplated, the man heard a faint car engine in the distance. The sound became louder as the vehicle drew nearer. Then he heard more engines. The drone increased in volume, as the apparent convoy descended into the field. The engines became a rumble, reverberating, just outside of the structure. He stood and faced the dull roar. Beams of bright light began to spear through the gaping planks of the barn. They were here.

To block the glare, the black man held up his hand, shielding his blinded eyes. His body, once more, began to revolt—heart racing, stomach churning, legs quivering. He walked to the door and peered out, squinting against the haze of light. Looking just above the lamps, avoiding the glare, Zadok calculated that there were approximately twenty vehicles lined up facing the barn. People were spilling from car doors and from truck beds. He noticed Stucky in his red cap perched atop the driver's seat of his '55 Ford Thunderbird. It was as though the crowd was lined up to watch a movie or a sporting event. This was merely a diversion for them.

Zadok recognized his three foes emerging from the crowd. Monty and Reggie strutted, side by side, towards the barn, while Arvis reluctantly trailed behind. As the trio neared the door, the black man retreated into the variegated light of the interior. The door creaked when the boys entered, dark silhouettes through the gaping entrance. Zadok could discern the grin on Monty's face. The boy led the way, halting next to a chunk of broken beam.

Picking up the club, the large young man tapped the end of the plank in his palm. "Ready for an ass-kickin', boy?"

From behind the leader, Reggie added, "Maybe after, we give your old lady another visit."

The black man could make out the boy's sinister leer.

Monty's body flickered as he passed through the shafts of light and shadow, creeping towards his opponent. The effect reminded Zadok of one of those rotating lampshades with cutouts that seemed to move when the light flickered through them. Monty swung his weapon like a pendulum. Halting before his nemesis, the young man eyed Zadok as though assessing him. Zadok straightened and lifted his chin. His arms were taut, and he clinched his fists. Otherwise, he didn't move or make a sound.

Reggie stood a few feet to Monty's right, flanking the leader.

Swinging the chunk of wood onto his broad shoulder, Monty grunted. "Well, boy, let's get this over with."

Light and shadow flashed before Zadok's eyes, when his foe lurched forward and whipped the weapon at him. The black man barely had time to throw his arm up in front of him. The wood crashed against his shoulder and splintered. Zadok realized how fortunate he was that the board was old and brittle. Lunging, he countered with a roundhouse punch that caught Monty on the jaw. The opponent's legs buckled, and the young man went limp, sinking to the ground. Ignoring the burning in his knuckles, the black man, filled with an adrenaline-charged rage, dropped and straddled the supine figure. He drew back his fist, preparing for another strike. From the corner of his eye, Zadok caught sight of Reggie, just before the boy collided into him.

The two rolled in the matted litter. Zadok was on his back, when Reggie scrambled over him and straddled his midsection. The boy cocked his fist. But, before the blow could slam into his face, the black man reached up and caught the plunging fist in a vise-like grip, like an eagle sinking its talons into its struggling prey.

In the eerie light, Zadok could make out his opponent's contorted grimace registering shock and pain. The boy pulled against his foe's hold. Suddenly, Zadok released his crushing grip. As Reggie's arm jerked away, the black man twisted his body and pitched his nemesis into the debris. Zadok sprang to his feet. Baring his white teeth, the man grabbed Reggie by his pompadour and yanked the boy to his feet. Zadok then slammed his tight fist squarely into his foe's face. His head jarred back, Reggie stumbled backwards, then collapsed.

Immediately following, the black man was jolted with a sharp pain in the middle of his back. Air rushed from his lungs, and Zadok dropped to one knee. He felt his opponent's weight bearing on him, as Monty pushed against his back, attempting to take the man all the way to the ground. Zadok turned on his knee and, twisting, swung his head under Monty's arm. Wrapping his strong arms around the black man, the boy locked his fingers under Zadok's chest, and laid his weight on the man. In a struggle to get his feet under him, the black man clasped Monty's waist and kicked his legs out, like a frog skimming over a pond. He scuffed up flakes of straw and a cloud of dust.

Finally, Zadok gained his feet and shoved against Monty's pressing bulk. Clasping his arms around the young man's thighs, Zadok strained and, with a mighty surge, straightened his aching legs. With Monty dangling over his shoulder, the black man felt himself tipping backward. The two hit the ground with a thud. The air was knocked out of Zadok. But he knew his opponent got the worst of it, for the black man landed on Monty's head and chest. Rolling to his hands and knees, Zadok gasped for air, then pushed himself up to his feet.

He took a moment to recover, and bent over, with his hands braced on his thighs. He waited until Monty turned over and rose to his hands and knees. Then Zadok leapt forward and whipped his boot into the young man's side. With a gasp, Monty collapsed onto his other side, and clutched his hands against the injured ribs. Then, as if punting a football, Zadok drove the toe of his boot into his foe's face. Letting out an anguished guttural cry, Monty's head lashed back. Blood spewed from his nose and mouth. The boy rolled onto his back and, cupping his hands over his face, rocked from side to side. Stepping between his opponent's feet, the black man delivered another kick and smashed his boot into the young man's groin. Monty curled up in the fetal position, moaning and grimacing in pain. His hands cradled his crotch, as the young man breathlessly groaned.

Before he could resume his assault, Zadok noticed, from the corner of his eye, Reggie had stirred. The brunette was turning onto his side. His foe strode over to him, leapt, and planted a heel into the boy's kidney. Arching his back, Reggie hollered. Next, Zadok stomped his boot into his opponent's ribs. Tightly tucking his arm against the damaged bones, Reggie rolled onto his back.

The black man straddled the boy and began slugging him in the face. His knuckles became slick, with blood.

Suddenly, Zadok was thrust into a murky world. A blast of pain jolted through his head, and white sparks whirled before his eyes. Except for the throbbing pain, the man was senseless. He felt as though he were floating, as he collapsed, face down, on the matted floor, sending up puffs of flakes and dust. All turned black. But he was aware of voices.

"Good work, Arvy!" Monty's voice sounded nasally and thick. "You're good for somethin' after all!"

"I had to; he was killing Reg!"

"Well, we're gonna kill him!"

The leader beckoned to his other partner. "Reg! Reggie! Jesus, he worked you over perty good!"

"Fuck! I think he broke my nose!" Reggie's voice sounded thick and nasally as well.

"No shit! Your face is covered in blood!"

"So is yours, Monty!" Arvis observed.

Reggie let out raspy moans. "I think that fucker broke my ribs too!" He snarled. "God damn him! I'm gonna kill that son of a bitch!"

Zadok heard more moaning and scuffling.

"Here. Easy, Reg," Monty suggested.

Then, addressing Arvis, the leader added, "Help me get him

up."

"God, my head hurts!" Reggie growled.

"So does mine," Monty grumbled.

So does mine, Zadok thought to himself.

As if reading the black man's mind, Monty echoed the thought, "So does his, I bet! Arvy nailed him with a piece of beam! Come on, let's stomp the bastard!"

Zadok felt the blows to his ribs and back, as the air was knocked out of him. He was breathless and couldn't move. The man was dazed. But somewhere, in the back of his mind, the black man was spurring himself to act. His body, however, wouldn't respond.

"Pick him up!"

Amid grunts, groans, and moans, Zadok felt hands tugging at his two hundred-plus pound frame.

"Come on, Arvy, help!"

The trio struggled with the man's bulk. Despite Monty and Reggie's pangs emanating from their bruised ribs and Arvy's reticence, they managed to lift Zadok to his feet. But the three had to support him, for their opponent was limp and practically dead weight. Monty awkwardly slugged Zadok in the stomach. It was just enough to knock the recovered wind out of their victim. The leader seemed frustrated with the weak blow, but he was straining under Zadok's weight. Monty stepped back, his left hand pressing against his foe's shoulder.

"Hold him!"

Reggie and Arvis grunted, while they strained under the burden. Drawing back, Monty slammed his fist into Zadok's cheek. Slack-jawed, the black man shook his throbbing head. Again, the leader cocked back his fist. But Zadok struggled through his stupor. And, before the punch could connect, the black man lunged forward, at an angle, jerking his tensed arms from his captors' grasp. He swung his arm over Monty's punch and caught the assailant's throat in the crook of his arm. Sidling behind the man, Zadok squeezed. Monty's fingers clawed at his foe's arm. But the black man dropped to his knees and squeezed ever tighter. To no avail, the gagging man thrashed and writhed, pumping his heels through the dried dung and straw. His struggles weakened, until the man was still.

Reggie stepped up and attempted to kick around the slumped leader, aiming for Zadok's head. The black man instantly released his hold on Monty and caught the speeding foot in his clutches. Climbing to his feet, Zadok pulled Reggie's leg taut, and planted a kick of his own into the boy's groin. With a wheeze, Reggie curled forward. Zadok released the captured foot, and his opponent dropped to one knee, cupping his loins. The black man drove his knee into Reggie's blood-smeared and swollen face. The boy's head flung back, and Zadok, once again, planted a kick into his foe's groin. Collapsing onto his butt, Reggie curled his legs to his chest, yet pressing his hands against his crotch.

The black man briefly glanced up at Arvis, who stood as though dumbfounded. Then the black man, again, launched into action. He drove the toe of his boot into Reggie's shielding hands. With a howl, the assailed jerked his hands away, and he wagged the injured hand in the air, as if attempting to shake off the pain. Then Zadok repeatedly kicked his nemesis in the groin until Reggie collapsed on his side.

Suddenly, the black man was jolted from behind, as Monty charged into him, clasping his arms in a bear hug, and pinning Zadok's arms to his sides. Maintaining his balance, the black man set his feet in a wide stance. He bent his knees and, violently, twisted from side to side, like a hooked trout fighting against a fishing line. Monty was thrown clear. As the boy stumbled backwards, Zadok was right on him. Before his opponent could regain his balance, the black man thrust his boot between Monty's legs. He continued to rapidly snap his foot into the slumped figure. As

Monty sank to his knees, Zadok gave a quick glance over to Arvis. The anxious boy remained passive. Zadok thrust his heel into Monty's bloodied and swollen face. The casualty fell onto his back. And the black man repeatedly stomped on the man's genitalia. With clenched teeth, Zadok unleashed his fury on the supine figure, relishing his foe's contorted expression of agony.

His rage did not ebb and, vehemently, he continued his onslaught, until Arvis once again crept up from behind. But Zadok had remained wary of the boy, anticipating the chance of another counter attack. Perhaps it was a slight sound or a flicker of shadow, but the black man sensed the impending assault. He spun around in time to spy the metal bucket that Arvis swung rushing at him. Zadok clasped the lip of the heavy pail. Using his body as a fulcrum, he pulled with the boy's momentum, throwing his attacker across the floor. Stumbling through the debris, Arvis dropped the bucket and skidded onto his knees. Zadok marched over and grabbed the back of the boy's collar. He jerked Arvis to his feet. Violently, the black man shook his terrified opponent.

Between clinch teeth, Zadok growled, "I know you didn't touch my wife that night, but you were there; you were there, and you stood by, while it happened! You watched and did nothing!"

With that, the black man gave the boy a powerful shove. The force propelled Arvis back across the floor, to the wall, where the ancient planks gave way to the impact of his body. The boy's butt wedged within the splintered slats.

Zadok's chest heaved with his panting breaths. All was otherwise silent, but for the pattering of fresh raindrops pelting the roof or darting past the gaping holes and splatting on the dusty floor. He barely noticed the drops that fell on him, as he surveyed the carnage; Reggie lay motionless on his side, and Monty was on his back, also quite still. The two seemed unconscious. He was finished. For the moment, his fury was spent. But the man's pain and exhaustion diminished, in his triumph. All of his frustration, anxiety, and fear were gone. Zadok wasn't even worried about what fate awaited him outside. He would take it as it came.

Shuffling to the door, the man stepped out into the haze of car lights. Raindrops twinkled in the glare. The spectators were little more than silhouettes within the brightness. Their ruckus quickly died when, one by one, the onlookers noticed Zadok plodding through the damp grass. He halted before the line of vehicles, and scanned the dark faces. There were a few muted utterances. Adjusting to the light, Zadok could discern some of the expressions of bewilderment in the visages that gawked back at him. Sapped of strength and emotion, Zadok hung his head and sank to his knees. He felt the moisture soak through his pant legs.

Two young men stepped from the crowd and strode past the kneeling black man, while approaching the barn. Zadok figured that this was it. But, at least he got his vengeance, for what it was worth.

Even so, the man didn't want it to end here; he wanted to return home to his family. What would become of them without him? They would make do. They were safe with his mother. They could go live with Tassy's parents. But Zadok wouldn't be there to watch his son grow into manhood; he wouldn't be there to admire his wife, as she went about her daily tasks or as she quietly sat, contemplating and dreaming. He wouldn't be there to hold her and to comfort her or she, him.

Someone yelled from the barn for help. And several people trotted past Zadok to the dilapidated building. Shortly, they passed him, returning as they packed the limp bodies of Monty and Reggie toward the fleet of vehicles. Arvis sheepishly followed. The rescuers lay their burdens on the wet ground. He stared as if in a dream, while a few people knelt beside the bodies, leaning over and assessing the casualties, or attempting to gently revive them. It all seemed unreal; a black man had badly beaten two white men. The unreal part would be if he walked away from the incident with his life—most unreal, if he walked away unpunished. But the man knew that there would be a reckoning. There would be hell to pay. And, considering that he was surrounded by so many white people, it would likely be almost immediate.

"They're still alive!" Zadok heard someone remark.

He felt a twinge of disappointment. The black man wished that they had died, since he, himself, would most likely be so soon. Many of the spectators stood with their blank stares fixed on Zadok. He heard grumbled remarks:

"Fuckin' nigger!"

"That black bastard is dead!"

"He's got to be crazy!"

A few began to slowly advance.

Anxiously, J.J. sped the cruiser over the highway, red light reflecting in the darkness, the siren blaring. Rain spattered against the windshield. The lawman hissed curses to himself. He had stopped at the burger stand in town for a cup of coffee and a maple bar, when he overheard a member of the kitchen crew telling the others that he had just got a call from Almaville; a crazy buck nigger went into the pool hall there and challenged the whole room to a fight!

"He's meetin' them at that old barn, just right outside o' town!"

The others remarked on the incredulous report.

J.J. left his order and jumped into his patrol car. That wasn't very long ago, by the time he heard the news, Zadok had already met his intended quarry and was already heading for the barn. Hopefully, there would be some preliminary trifling before the combat began.

He felt a mixture of relief and uncertainty, when the Almaville welcome sign came into view. Looking to his right, J.J. could see the barn. A sheet of light was cast over the strip of field before the ancient structure. He realized that a line of cars faced the building. The tires screeched as the deputy cranked the wheel and slid onto the shoulder of the highway. The cruiser bounced down the grassy slope that dropped to the meadow. He felt as though he were racing a power boat over rough water, as the car bounced over the uneven ground.

He could make out a kneeling figure in the haze—Zadok, no doubt. Others milled about the fleet of vehicles. Some were approaching Zadok. As he drew nearer, the lawman discerned two figures lying on the ground. A few people were bent over the bodies, apparently tending to them. He could make out the black man's indifferent expression and the grim looks of those who approached him.

The latter retreated, as the cruiser threateningly bore down on them. J.J. hit the brakes and skidded to a halt. The car served as shield between the crowd and the black man. Flinging open the door, the lawman leapt from the cruiser.

He bellowed, across the hood, at the crowd, "Ya'll stay back, now! This man is in my custody!"

A low din rose. A voice demanded an ambulance for the two beaten boys.

"I'll take care of it!" J. J. assured. He turned to his kneeling friend. He helped Zadok to his feet. "You alright?"

"Yes."

The deputy assessed the black man's face. "You got beat up some."

Zadok gave a half-hearted smile. "Some."

He rubbed his damp knees. "Glad to see you though."

"Yeah, if Sheriff Platt were here, he'd a let 'em have ya."

He took his handcuffs from his belt. "I gotta cuff ya."

Zadok turned his back and placed his hands behind him. But J.J. turned his charge full circle, then placed the man's hands before him. The deputy clasped the handcuffs around Zadok's wrists. He directed his charge to the front passenger's door.

"This man is under arrest!" he announced to the grumbling crowd.

Climbing into the cruiser, J.J. ignored the demanding inquires cast, at him.

"Hey, what about Monty and Reg?"

"Did you call the ambulance!"

"Where you takin' 'im?"

Braving the disgruntled onlookers, the lawman opened the passenger's door, and Zadok eagerly slid into the seat.

"Why you puttin' a nigger in the front seat?"

J.J. walked back around the front of the cruiser and climbed in. Slamming his door, the deputy spun the car in a half-circle, and sped towards the highway. As the cruiser bounced, J.J. slowed the vehicle.

"I can't believe it, Zadok," he grumbled. "I'm surprised you aren't dead!"

"Me too." Zadok grinned.

They fell quiet for a moment.

Then, the black man added, "I might've been had you not shown up when you did!"

Glancing over to his charge, the lawman raised his brows and flashed a grin.

Then he radioed the Almaville Medical Clinic and requested medical assistance, for two battered men.

When asked for details, J.J. casually replied. "I don't know how bad they've been beaten. But there are people with them, and, as I say, they're near the barn outside of town."

At the edge of the field, the deputy stopped the car and removed the handcuffs from Zadok's wrists. Tossing the cuffs up on the dashboard, he accelerated up the bank. Then he headed down the highway.

J. J. chided his charge, "You know this isn't over, don't you?"

He looked over to the silent passenger and added, "You're gonna have to leave town right away—unless you've got another trick up your sleeve!" He referred to the incident concerning Osmond Royal.

Zadok knowingly smirked.

The lawman snorted. "Looks like you nearly killed those boys! There'll be hell to pay!"

The black man remained silent.

Frowning, J.J. exclaimed, "Are you listening, Zadok! I've grown to like you, man! I don't wanna see you die!"

His charge turned to him and presented a serene smile.

"What?" the driver demanded.

Gazing out of the windshield, Zadok replied, "The first thing I'm going to do is go back to my family. I'll have to get my pick up running." He snorted. "I don't think I'll be allowed to ride the bus anymore."

"Bullshit!" J.J. barked. "I'll drive you to your mother's place. And I'll get your pickup taken care of."

With sincere gratitude, Zadok turned and smiled. "Thank you."

Suddenly, the passenger wrinkled his nose. "How'd you know where to find me?"

The deputy explained about overhearing the conversation at the burger stand.

The two were silent.

Then J. J. spoke, "You just better hope those boys don't die or end up crippled! They'll hunt you down and rip you apart, like a hog come to butcher!"

He sighed. "Man, with all the trouble that you've heaped on your head, tell me, Zadok, was it worth it?"

The black man turned to the driver. His serene smile broadened.

"Yes," he replied, "it was worth it."

J.J. pulled up to the white picket fence in his '57 Corvette. He found Zadok and Gideon in the yard, with a fluffy gray pup. As the lawman stepped out of his car, the father and son turned from their recreation and met J. J. at the gate. He was casually dressed. The man donned a white t-shirt, denim jeans, and tennis shoes. He held an avocado green cardboard box in his hand.

"How ya doin', Zade?"

"Just fine, J.J. And you?"

"Good. How are the ribs?"

"They feel fine."

The young dog gamboled up to the visitor, leaped about, and pawed at J.J.'s knee.

"Cute pup," the visitor observed.

"Yeah," Gideon replied. "She's going to be big! She's called a Caucasian shepherd. She's only eight weeks old!"

Impressed, the man raised his brows. "Man, she is big! Where did you get such a dog?"

"Grandma knows an artist who breeds 'em. She got her to re-place Duke!"

"Well, that's fine!"

The visitor offered his host the box. "Oh, here, Zade. I've got something, for you."

Taking the box, the black man lifted the lid and found a stack of cash. J.J. grinned while watching his host's eyes widen.

He explained, "Some of the folks took a collection for you. They figured you might be out of work for a time. There's $200 there. That should get you by for about a month."

Gideon's eyes bulged, and his mouth puckered into an "o".

J.J. went on, "Mostly farmers you've done work for, a couple of merchants."

Arching a brow, Zadok eyed his guest. "And how much did you put in?"

Feigning offense, J. J. knitted his brows. "Hey, I saved your ass outside Almaville! I got your truck running and back to you! What more do you expect?"

"I expect that you put in a good chunk of this money."

"Hey," the visitor shrugged, "I'm a bachelor. My house was inherited; my car is paid for. My only vice is women."

His host clapped him on the shoulder.

"Well," Zadok commented, "I couldn't be idle for a whole month. But this is wonderful. Thank everyone for me." He squeezed J.J.'s shoulder. "And thank you."

The host led his guest to the porch. "Come on in. Tassy and Mama are eager to see you again."

"How is your family?"

The two stood at the door.

Eyes sparkling, Zadok answered, "Tassy is doing much better. She's a strong gal." He sighed. "We haven't—well, it's just enough to hold her and kiss her. I want to give her the time she needs."

Arching a brow, J.J. suggested, "Maybe she's trying to give you the time you need."

The black man frowned. "Time—for what?"

The visitor shrugged. "Maybe time to accept her again; time to deal with the fact that she was misused."

Zadok glared. "I don't need time for that! I want her! I love her! She's still the same woman I fell in love with and married!"

Again, J. J. shrugged. "Maybe you should tell her that; maybe you should discuss it with her."

The host pursed his lips then replied, "I will. But I want to wait until she's ready."

From the corner of his eye, the guest peered at the other. "Sounds like the two of you are doing a lot of waiting. You might just be wasting precious time."

"It doesn't matter. All that matters is Tassy. I can wait."

J.J.'s admiration showed in his smile.

He went on to another subject. "There's been quite a ruckus in town. Those two boys you near beat to death, their parents came to the office."

Zadok gave his guest his grave attention.

"Yeah," J.J. continued, "they came in wanting to know what I was gonna do about you. But I told them you had disappeared— you know, tryin' to play up the mystical angle, fire from the sky and all. That Mrs. Brisby scoffed. But I told her to try telling that to the kluxes.

"Dinmont suggested calling in Chief Miggs. I told him if the chief could find you, he was welcome to you. Then Dinmont said that he better not hear that I was helpin' you." The deputy's eyes hardened. "I told him not to fuckin' threaten me in my own office. Then I ran 'em off."

He smirked. "When Sheriff Platt returned, he chewed me a new asshole. But he seemed more upset about those boys coming into his town and causing trouble. He seems to have some kind of respect for you and Tassy, despite his racist disposition."

"How about that," Zadok mused.

J.J. continued, "Them kluxes still can't figure you out. They are afraid. Them bastards aren't use to any opposition when they wreak their righteous wrath. You threw 'em for a loop! By the way, Ozzie shot himself in the head night 'fore last. Didn't kill himself though. Looks like he's gonna be a turnip for the rest of his sorry life."

Again, J. J. smirked, then added, "And you'll probably be pleased to know that the doc had to castrate Monty. Some kind of infection set in, I guess. Anyway, he'll probably end up shooting himself too. I know I would."

The guest smiled. "Reggie kept his goods, but who knows

when he'll feel like using them again."

His blue eyes glinted. "I think you taught 'em their lesson, Zade."

Folding his arms, J.J. leaned against the post. "You're gonna have to stay out of town. I would move out of the area if I were you."

His host sighed. "We thought about going to California. Tassy's parents live there. But we might just stay with Mama, for a time, if I can find enough work."

"Well, if there's anything I can do, I'll do it," his visitor offered. "Haul some of your stuff from your place, or whatever."

Laying his hand on J.J.'s shoulder, Zadok replied, "Thanks, J.J. You don't know how much I appreciate that."

"Well, you can show your appreciation by feeding me." The guest grinned.

His host slapped him on the back and returned the grin. "Alright. Let's go inside."

As Zadok opened the door, the aroma of pot roast and biscuits wafted into the outside air. J. J. felt his mouth water.

Tassy stepped out from the kitchen. Her beautiful face seemed to light up. She gave an enchanting smile, while she welcomed the visitor.

As they embraced, the woman declared, "Jasper, it is so good to see you again!"

The man noted how Tassy had adopted her mother-in-law's compromise; when they first met at Mother Quarry's house, the day he returned Zadok's pickup, the old woman called him Mr. White. The lawman insisted she call him J.J. Mother Quarry offered to call him Jasper. He remembered the old woman from his childhood. She had had some association with his mother and grandmother.

Clasping the back of his arm, his hostess led J.J. into the kitchen, where he found Mother Quarry tending to the stove.

When the woman noticed the guest, she lit up.

"Jasper! You are right on time! Supper is about ready! Come! Have a seat!"

"Thank you, Mother Quarry."

Tassy pulled out a chair from one end of the table. "Here, Jasper."

The man took heed of her.

Mother Quarry brought a bowl of corncobs to the table. "How is your mama, Jasper?"

"She's fine. Kennett seems to suit her."

"She's been there, how long?"

"Almost four years now."

As the old woman retrieved the biscuits, Tassy offered, "Would you like something to drink, Jasper—coffee, tea, lemonade?"

"Lemonade please. It was a warm drive."

Setting the bowl of steaming biscuits on the table, the old woman told her son to call in Gideon.

"And remind him to leave that pup outside."

Receiving his glass of lemonade, J.J. looked at the pot roast as Mother Quarry brought it to the table. The pleasing aromas filled his nostrils, and his mouth watered. One by one, the family took their seats about the table.

Once they were all settled, Zadok looked over to the guest. "J.J., would you mind saying the blessing?"

Hesitantly, the man nodded. He wasn't a religious person. He hadn't a definite conviction of who or what God might be, and he rarely gave the idea any thought.

As he looked over each member of the family, their heads bowed and eyes closed, he thought of how good and decent these people were. He reflected upon the trouble and tribulations they had endured over the past several days. He thought about the townsfolk, their attitudes and behaviors, and about the social barriers between black and white citizens. He considered the stupidity of judging people by the color of their skin rather than by the character of their hearts, about the general air of ignorance and injustice.

And finally, the guest offered the words that came to mind. He prayed, "God, help us."